GEORGE: THE LONG ROAD AHEAD

SCARLET LE CLAIR

mina,

Hope you enjoy the journey

Scarlet ♡

Published by Scarlet Le Clair 2016
Edited: Kirsty Turner
Cover design: Mina Carter
Model: Phil Bruce
Formatting by Abigail Davies at Pink Elephant Designs
All Rights Reserved

PROLOGUE

I don't remember a lot after leaving Poppy's bedroom. The sound of the gun was still ringing in my ears. Will and Adam came to help me up, I remember that, gently lifting me up off the bed and supporting me the best they could down the stairs. My head hung low, my eyes felt unfocussed, just watching my feet move one in front of the other. The military guys surrounded me as we left the house and I recall them talking to each other. Some sort of code, as they checked our escape route. I didn't care, couldn't care. The zombies could come in hordes around the corner and rip me to shreds, tearing off my flesh like it was pulled pork. It was only what I deserved. I understood why Kelly had done it, why she had taken my kids away but I was still angry at her. Angry at myself for leaving her so long that she felt she had no other way out, but to kill my children and herself.

Adam and Will had explained that she had passed away, before they had chance to take her down to the car. She had fallen asleep and not woken back up. That they had taken care of her the whole time. I knew what that meant; a bullet to the brain, for each of my children and my beautiful wife.

1

I understood, I preferred that than to see them rise again, their lifeless eyes staring at me as the shell of their once gorgeous little faces tried to have me for dinner.

I let them put me back into the jeep and watched with unseeing eyes as they moved quickly back into my house and out again. Carrying two small bodies wrapped in sheets.

I placed my head against the cool glass of the car window as we drove back to the military compound.

My mind racing with what ifs and maybe's. What the hell was I supposed to do now? There was no point in going on. My family, my whole world was gone.

Pain tore through every fiber of my being, my chest ached so badly, and my throat constricted so that I couldn't breathe or swallow. My eyes blinded by tears. This was what I deserved, why should I keep breathing when they hadn't.

After what seemed like minutes we had pulled up just inside the compound gates. I blinked away the tears, surprised by how we had gotten back so quickly.

I opened the door on autopilot, getting out slowly. I wasn't sure what to do, where to go. Did I even belong anywhere anymore?

I just stood at the side of the car, watching as the men unloaded their gear and the lifeless forms of my family.

"George," I heard my voice being called but it was like I was underwater, all muffled and unclear.

"George?" there it was again. I tried to look towards the sound, but my eyes were unfocused, my legs felt like jelly.

I could see the floor coming up to meet my face, and I couldn't even bring myself to care. I just let myself fall, before strong arms wrapped around me and lifted me up.

"Come on Bud, I've got you," Wills deep voice was warm and caring and provided a little comfort. He led me towards a huge building, my feet dragging along, feeling like the had a ton of bricks attached to them. Not wanting to cooperate.

"George, are you ok?" Nia's lovely face appeared in front of mine and I realized that it was her voice I could hear when I stepped out of the car.

I watched as Will shook his head no to her, and the look of pity in her eyes as she covered her mouth with her hands was almost too much to see.

"Just need to lie down," I gasped out, each word seemed to echo through my head which was already spinning.

"Ok, follow me I'll show you to where the captain has given us all rooms." She turned on her heel and led the way into the building.

Even now I couldn't tell you the route we took or the people we saw on the way. I kept my head down, focused on Nia's black boots in front of us.

I was scared to pick my head up, to look people in the eye. Lest they see the monster I was, the man who had left his wife and children to die. So terrified that she had seen no other way out than to put herself and the kids to sleep; permanently.

We stopped suddenly outside of a door in a long corridor, "This is your room George, Will is just down the hallway as is Billy."

I mumbled some variety of thanks and swung open the door.

"Can we get you anything?" Nia's sweet voice asked. But I could hear the sympathy in her voice. I knew that concern would mar her pretty face. Something that I didn't need.

"No, I'm good." Without saying anything else I closed the door on their faces. Not wanting anymore company. I just needed to be alone.

I didn't even bother to look around the room, I spotted the bed in the right hand far corner and got into it. Under the scratchy covers, fully clothed and booted.

It was only then that I let out the pain, I started to cry until everything went black.

CHAPTER ONE

It had been three days since we returned from the horror show that was my home. Three, long ass days. It felt more like a lifetime. I'd barely left the tiny room that the military had assigned to me. I felt numb to everyone and everything around me, I didn't want their sympathy and pitying looks. I didn't want their hugs and kind words. I wanted my family back, I wanted to see Poppy's smile again, to hear Cameron's little laugh. To see my beautiful wife again, to feel her touch, to hold the three of them in my arms. I paced my room, back at the Army's compound. The bile rose in my throat. Anger and guilt started to take over again, it never left I'm not sure that it ever would.

"AHHHHH," I turned and punched the door, leaving a dent in the dark wood, but the pain radiating through my fist, my knuckles, felt good. A welcome distraction from the pain inside my chest.

A small knock at the door, had me coming back to myself "What?" I roared.

The door opened and Nia came in, she wore black jeans and a tight black vest top. Her dark hair flowed in loose curls around her shoulders, olive green eyes looked at me with concern, before dropping to my chest and back up again.

"We're ready," her voice was low and quiet, as if she would scare me away if she spoke normally.

My eyes met hers and hers filled up, I closed mine and pumped my fist, noting that nothing felt broken, but that there was a lot of pain.

"I'll be right there, thank you," It came out as a hoarse whisper, my throat was sore from crying. I didn't mean to take my anger out on her, or on any of them but I couldn't seem to control it so it was easier to block them out.

She didn't reply, when I heard the click of the door being closed behind her I opened my eyes. Leaving me alone in my painful abyss once more. I hated pushing her away, but I couldn't let anyone get close ever again. My grief was helping me to build walls around my heart. I kept telling myself that it would be easier, if someone else got hurt then it was better for me not to feel. I could be more objective and less emotional on missions too.

I was about to leave when I realised that I was only wearing my red boxer shorts and nothing else, I sorted through the clothes that Captain Cooper's men had brought for me on auto pilot. Picking out some black combat trousers and a dark grey vest top, with black boots.

I got dressed, taking my time and walked slowly out of the building, passed the canteen. The smell of food both making me feel hungry and nauseous at the same time. My feet felt like they were lead weights and I was dragging them along.

As usual I ignored everyone I passed, keeping my head down, concentrating on placing one foot after another. Not wanting to get to my destination but knowing that I needed to, that if I didn't do it then I would regret it forever.

I finally arrived at the makeshift graveyard right at the back of the compound, my head bowed, I closed my eyes and steeled myself for what was about to happen. I took a deep breath and raised my head to face my friends, Will, Nia, Adam, Amelia and Billy were there amongst others we helped to save from Deacon, all dressed in as dark colours as they could find. Captain Cooper and a few of his men had come too. But the only thing I could focus on was the three bodies wrapped in white sheets under a massive old oak tree. The huge branches forming a leafy canopy for them, the two of them looked so tiny, even Kelly my sweet sweet wife looked small. I had tried to be mad at her, tried to hate her for taking away our children, but she did what she felt she needed to do to protect them from the undead horrors that awaited them.

Instead I turned my anger towards Deacon and his men, the way I saw it, they kept me away from my loved ones. I reserved some anger for myself also, I should have tried harder to get back to them, should have fought to leave everyone else behind and get back to the ones that depended on me.

I nodded and the Captain started to say a few words as they lowered Kelly, I walked closer meeting Amelia at the side of the grave, she wore a navy knee length dress and held some brightly coloured wild flowers that she and Nia had picked this morning whilst Will, Adam and I dug the graves.

She handed them to me and placed her hand on my arm, I flinched at the physical contact. She removed her hand quickly and went to stand by Adams side. I waited for the Captain to stop talking and then dropped in the flowers all but two of them. I kept a purple one for Poppy and a blue one for Cameron. My hands shook wildly, and I held on to the flowers tightly, crushing their stems. I said a silent goodbye, my throat constricting so tightly I couldn't form the words out loud.

As Will and Adam lowered in the bodies of my children, my legs gave way, barely registering the sting on my knees from hitting the ground hard as deep gut wrenching sobs tore through my body. I couldn't catch a breath, I wished that Adam had let me die alone in Poppy's room.

Now though I swore that they would pay, the zombies and the rest of Deacons crew. I would hunt them down and kill as many of them as possible.

I asked that the children be buried together so that they would not be alone, out of my trousers pocket I pulled Cameron's favorite toy, a red sports car and Poppy's small pink teddy bear. Taking deep breaths to try to calm the sobs, I staggered to my feet and dropped their toys in with them along with the flowers.

"See you soon kids" I whispered, my heart was broken in three, my chest felt like it was being ripped open, I didn't think the pain could get any worse. I closed my eyes wanting to block out the world, needing to be alone in my grief. The tears kept falling, seemingly never-ending.

A strong hand grabbed my left arm, Will was helping me to stay on my feet. A small hand slipped into mine and squeezed it, I smelled the scent of vanilla and knew that it was Nia who stood on the other side of me.

The Captain finished his speech for the children and gave a nod. Will let go of me. He and Adam picked up the shovels they had placed in the ground and started to fill in the graves. Thud. Thud, Thud as the dirt hit the bodies below.

My legs gave way again, my strength gone, days of no sleep, the pain and hurt, all coming together at once to take me down. Nia collapsed with me and I sobbed into her shoulder. My tears soaking into her top. She hugged me and stroked my hair, pulling me into her, I felt the warmth of her body, the hard contours of it from months of starving and being on the run.

"I'm sorry George, so so sorry," she kept repeating over and over.

Images of Kelly and I dancing at our wedding came back to me, our first dance, her body pressed against mine. She was softer and rounder than Nia but she was four months pregnant with Poppy at the time. I remember the love that surrounded us that day, how happy we both were and how her smile had made my life so much brighter.

Shame enveloped me, I had chosen to help save the lives of strangers instead of getting back to my family sooner. If I wasn't lying in a sleeping bag with another woman, then maybe my wife and children would still be here.

"No!!" I screamed, scaring Nia and pushing her away. I jumped to my feet, staggering backwards, seeing the fear in Nia's eyes almost floored me again but this time my legs held me. I turned and ran as fast as I could. I ignored the calls of my friends, blocked out their worried voices. I can't remember how I got back to my room, the next thing I do remember was closing and locking the door behind me, spinning in circles looking at the plain white walls but that's all I could see was the faces of my children, of Kelly crying out to me to help them.

I sat on my bed and reached for the faded green duffle bag underneath, it contained the bottle of whisky that was supposed to be for Deacon but was now mine, I opened it and took a deep long pull. I savored the flavor, the burn as it ran down my throat.

I lay back, the mattress was thin and hard beneath the rough grey covers, hearing the cries of my kids over and over. Tears soaked my pillow, my chest and ribs hurt from sobbing so hard. I continued to drink until eventually I cried myself into a drunken stupor, and passed out, fully dressed.

When I woke up it was the following morning. The rest of the day I alternated between finishing the bottle of whisky and sleeping. It was the only thing that could make the pain lesser. Although the nightmares had started to invade my sleep. Where I was forced to watch as my family got eaten as Deacon held me so that I couldn't move to help them. I woke up two days after the funeral, empty bottle by my side, still wearing the same clothes.

My mouth was dry, my head was throbbing, it hurt and there was a loud banging. I rolled over and tried to sit up. I realised that the banging was coming from my door and not inside of my head.

"George? I'm sorry man we need you, there's been a breach." Billy's panicked voice came through the door.

That cleared up my head, I was out of bed and grabbing my gun off a small table next to my bed, that and the red hard plastic chair were the only other pieces of furniture in here. I kept my clothes in the duffle bag, ready to leave at any moment.

I grabbed the jug of water off the table and filled a glass, my hands shook so badly that I spilled lots of the precious liquid over the table and onto the floor. I downed the glass in one not caring that it was now stale and ran to my door. Flinging it open and startling Billy, who jumped backwards. He wore a military uniform, I made a note to ask him about it later. I noticed his hair had been shaved close too and he now held himself with an air of confidence.

He quickly recovered, "It's the side gate over at the sister compound. A few dozen have broken through," Billy filled me in whilst walking away, knowing I would follow.

We walked briskly down the grey painted concrete corridors, people were moving about quickly but there was no panic, I took that as a good sign. These military men and women were trained to protect, to keep calm. It was an organized chaos. Because the public living area was full, captain Cooper and his men had set us up in their military living quarters.

This sister site that had been attacked was going to be a new living area, the plan was to start rescue missions again, but to bring more people in we needed more room. There was a small crew over there clearing out a huge warehouse and securing the fences. Making it a habitable place.

I didn't know much more than that, I hadn't really been a part of anything since we got back, I just lay in my room, not talking to anyone and barely eating. Nia and Will had tried but were now giving me the space that I needed.

Billy and I exited the building into the bright sunlight causing me to squint a little until my eyes adjusted.

Will bumped into me from behind, grabbing my arm he started to pull me along at a run.

"Will, what the….?"

"Nia was in there George," I heard the worry in his voice and suddenly fear replaced the anger I felt.

No, no, not again, please God, I can't lose anyone else, especially not her, I prayed to myself as the three of us ran at full speed towards the large open gates.

CHAPTER TWO

Adrenaline pumped through my system, and I forced myself to run faster, I overtook Will and got my gun ready. It was surprising how easily this came to me now. Captain Cooper's men were already at the scene, barking orders, moving efficiently through the chaos, loud gunshots echoing all around me. It looked like the people working there had been caught by surprise, I spun around in circles looking for Nia. I could see the men covering up the three dead, but refused to believe that she was one of those, so instead I focused on the living.

The military men were herding together the survivors; they would have to be thoroughly checked for bites or scratches and then put into a twenty-four-hour quarantine.

There were only four people in line being checked over, Amelia was one of them, I jogged over to her and gave her a hug. Happy to see her safe and hoping that she was not infected.

"Amelia, where is Nia?" desperation laced my voice, my heart felt like it was in my mouth and I found it hard to breathe.

"Uh, I don't know, there was so much going on and we got separated. She tried to lead them away from the rest of us. It didn't work, they kept coming. That was the last I saw of her. She was in the building." Amelia pointed to the large red-bricked warehouse that would hopefully become extra living quarters for new survivors. Amelia's lip started to quiver and she broke down into sobs.

The nurse checking her over, gave her the all clear for any bites or scratches and then led her back to the main compound where her and the others would be put into separate rooms, used for quarantine. They would be observed for twenty-four hours and then if still not showing any signs of the zombie virus they would be released back into the rest of our populace.

The pop of a gunshot was heard coming from inside the building and suddenly my legs were propelling me forward at top speed. Heading into the dark, ominous looking property, followed closely by Will and Adam. The stale damp smell of a long-abandoned building hit me, it wasn't pleasant but I ignored it, instead focusing on getting my eyes used to the darkness.

"Nia?" I called not caring who or what heard me. We were standing in what used to be a warehouse, what it distributed I didn't know and didn't care. There were multiple red doors that lined the light grey walls on this floor.

"George, you take the bottom floor, Billy and I will take the second floor." I nodded to Will as two military men came in the doors we had entered through carrying large, heavy looking torches.

One followed me and the other followed Will. I noted that they didn't offer to go up ahead and keep us civilians safe.

We walked quickly, desperate to find her alive and unharmed, I stayed alert my eyes darting all over the area, my ears trying to pick up the tiniest of sounds. We checked every room as we went, several pump trucks, empty pallets, and fork-lifts were lined against the right-hand wall. Long rows of red metal shelving units from floor to ceiling held various sized boxes. Private Lewis checked the area in-between the storage shelves. I could see an office at the back of the storage area. The torch Private Lewis held, highlighted small reddish-brown stains leading towards it, I broke into a run not bothering to check the rest of the doors or wait for the others.

I could now hear them, moaning and grunting, there were two of them trying to get past a barricade of office furniture. They were so focused on their prize that they didn't notice me behind them. I lifted my gun and shot them both at close range, in the heads, not missing.

"Nia!" I called, trying my hardest to push the furniture out of the way. Fear gripped my heart tightly until I thought it would burst, I was scared at what I would find inside.

"George?" I heard her small voice, coming from around the side of the office, I followed the sweet sound to see her shakily climbing up behind the sliding office window. I helped her through, and before her feet touched the ground the military man had his gun pointed on her.

"Don't move, miss, I'll need to take you to quarantine." He barked.

I ignored him in favor of checking her over. I saw that Nia's leg was bleeding, I stood in front of her so that my body was shielding her from the man. I could see the rest of our rescue party heading towards us. I could feel her starting to sway and I knew that she needed medical care asap. I spun towards private Lewis.

"Get your gun off her, now!" I told him through gritted teeth, Nia clung tightly to my back, she was shaking and the little whimpering noises coming from her mouth only fueled my anger more.

"Bbb but she's bleeding, we need to take her for a check-up

and into quarantine," he stammered. He was a tall man but stick thin, his military uniform hung off him. His dirty blonde hair was thinning on top and he had little beady eyes. They reminded me of Deacon and I immediately took a disliking to him.

I pointed my gun back at him and we had a standoff, "get that damn thing off her, now!" I shouted the last part, he looked wearily at me but lowered his weapon.

"George?" Nia's voice was real quiet, I turned to her as she let go of my shirt and just in time to catch her.

"Nia," Will's panic, cut through me like fire through ice, I dropped my gun, the metal hitting the cold concrete sounded too loud as it echoed off the walls.

I swept her up and into my arms, moving as fast as I possibly could to the tent that they had set up to check on the casualties. My legs burned but I pushed through it.

"We need a doctor," I called, the leg of Nia's Jeans was soaked in blood.

The doctor and her team, placed Nia on a gurney, strapped her down and covered her in a blanket. They began to wheel her to the medical area just off the side of the main building in our compound. I placed both my hands on my head, no not Nia. I needed to go with her, be near her when she woke up.

I tried to follow, but lieutenant Jacks stepped in front of me

"Sir, Captain Cooper asked me to ask if you would help to secure this compound. He requested the help of yourself and Mr. Perry."

"But, my friend is hurt, I want to make sure..." I started angrily trying to sidestep him.

"Yes. Sir I know, but this is important for the whole community. Please?" he had a determined look in his eyes. I was just about to argue again when a large hand clasped onto my shoulder.

"We got this, right George? We can do a good sweep, assess

the damage and then go see Nia. She will be out of it for a while. Let's let the doctors do their job."

"I still don't see why it needs to be us," yes, I knew that I sounded like a child and that I was pouting.

I knew that Will wanted to go and see Nia much more than I did, she was the only real family he had left, I considered his eyes and could see the pain in them.

But I knew that he would put the needs of the camp before his own needs as he knew I would too.

"Maybe I'm sick of putting others before the ones I love, Will." I spat out.

He winced at my words "George I-"

I immediately felt bad, it wasn't his fault that I had lost my family, I had saved many more lives by sticking around with Deacons crew, some of who now were my family. But nothing would make up for the loss of my wife and children.

I sighed and shrugged my shoulders "Ok then let's go, Billy, would you mind taking a walkie to the medical wing and letting us know of any ... complications?" He nodded and looked scared, but took the walkie offered to him by Lt. Jacks who gave me another. We all knew that complications meant being bitten. We knew that she was badly injured but not what had caused it.

Lt Jacks motioned to the table at the back of the room, on it was a roughly drawn map of the compound they aptly named, living quarters 2.

"Ok so I know you've been inside the building, that's been secured now. What we need to do is secure the exterior, see what fences need fixing and get some ideas on how to create a safe passage between the two compounds. We really need all hands-on deck for this."

"Why us?" I didn't understand why the Captain had requested us to help when he had so many men at his disposal

"I'm not sure, everyone has a job here. You must have said

or done something to allow the captain to trust your judgement. Perhaps he just wants to see what you can do? I've been with the Captain long enough to know that everything he does has a reason."

"Ok, George and I will go with you quickly and then report back to Captain Cooper but then I want to see my niece. Understood?" Will used his no-nonsense voice, and crossed his arms, challenging the Lt. to argue.

"Yes sir, understood." The soldier nodded and signaled to the other guards that we were heading out.

We walked around the perimeter, checking the stability of the fence and noting any weak points, Lt. Jacks marked the areas on a smaller map drawn into a notebook and wrote notes. As we walked, Jacks kept Will talking by discussing the plans for the area. Pointing out where they thought would be a good place to grow crops, where they would set up new class rooms for the children, and finally the point that they would like to use as a fenced in run way between the two areas so it would be safe to travel between the two compounds.

I kept quiet, in my head I kept hearing Nia, calling my name, screaming as a pus-filled zombie ripped shreds of skin off her arms. Once again, I was not there to keep her safe. But she's not harmed, she's safe and well in the infirmary I kept reminding myself.

Whilst the soldier and Will discussed ways to raise a fence and what materials they would need to re enforce it, I looked around. I could see a town in the distance, most of the food would probably be gone but we could possibly check it out for materials and other useful items but then realised that a town that close to camp would have already been checked by Captain Coopers men.

"George? That ok with you?" Will looked at me expectantly.

I nodded, running my hands through my dark hair, I just wanted to get back to Nia. "Yeah sounds good, Lt. could you take the plans back to Captain Cooper? Now if you don't mind I'm going to go see my friend," before waiting on his reply I turned and stalked back to the main compound. Going straight to the medical wing to the side of the main building.

"Sir, you can't come in here," The nurse called out from behind her desk. I kept walking towards her but she didn't back down. She was tall and awfully thin; her light hair was cut short and spiked. But it suited her delicate features.

"Sir please."

"Listen, nurse?" I waited for her response

"Amy," she replied firmly.

"Nurse Amy, please my friend was attacked, just yesterday I buried my whole family out under the trees in our cemetery, I can't lose another person that I love, I just can't. Please let me see her," my whole body shook as the tears threatened to come again, to overwhelm me. She looked into my eyes for a few moments, then nodded but did not move.

"She's still in surgery, take a seat in the waiting room and I'll ask the doctor to come and see you when she gets out." She patted my arm.

"Was she......bitten?" I gulped and closed my eyes both wanting a reply and not.

"No, it didn't look like it. But she has sliced her leg up badly. Once out of surgery we will put her in a room of her own for twenty-four hours just for security measures but we will know more once the doctor has finished." The nurse gave me a warm smile and gestured again to the small waiting room on my right. Billy was already sat in there, on the blue hard plastic chair, head in his hands.

Will came in seconds later followed by Adam

"How's Amelia?" I asked Adam.

She's good, they gave her the all clear but she still must wait out quarantine like the rest. We lost another two..." he trailed off at the end, dipping his head.

My heart ached, any loss of human life was a tragedy, we were losing this war against the undead. When he lifted his head, my gaze met his, shifting mine to Billy and then Will I knew that we would fight until the end, we would not go down easy.

"What's the news with Nia?" Adam asked going to sit opposite Billy.

"We don't really know a lot except that it's her leg, it's not a bite, but it requires surgery." I explained letting out a frustrated sigh. Not being able to see her was hard, I felt a pang of regret that I'd been ignoring them for the last few days.

"Ok that's good, well not good but good you know?" Adam looked at me for help, I don't think the poor boy knew what he was saying by the end of his sentence.

Despite the grim situation and the loss, we all felt, I started to laugh, soon the others joined in. We laughed and laughed, my ribs and jaw ached from laughing so much, but damn it felt good, I hadn't laughed like that in a long time, I don't think any of us had. As it wore off, I wiped tears from my eyes, the good type of tears this time.

"I so needed that," Will admitted, he looked straight at me, his jade green eyes burning into my soul. He knew that I needed it as well.

What I didn't need was the rush of guilt that washed over me, a wave of grief hitting me in the chest like a slab of concrete, making it so that I couldn't breathe. I had buried my entire family the day before yet here I was laughing it up with my boys, like I hadn't a care in the world.

I suddenly felt the room was getting much smaller, the walls, floors and ceilings were closing in on me. "I uh, I need to go, see you later," I mumbled.

I ignored the worried calls from Will and Adam and sped out of the building, and over to the small out building they used as an armory. I asked the bulky, bald, mean looking guard what was a good gun to use for practice. He grunted at me, handed over a gun and pointed to the sheet in front of him. I signed out what I was told was a SA80 A2 then exited around the side of the building where I could see a few shamblers, pushing up against the fence.

I walked closer to the fence. Calmed myself, took a deep breath, and lined up the shot on the first of the moaning undead. I wasn't sure of the gender. All traces of hair were gone, it wore no shirt, the chest cavity had been ripped open, and although I wasn't close enough, it didn't look as if any of the soft organs were still inside. Ripped denim jeans still clung to its legs, looking stiff with blood, mud and other bodily fluids. Arm outstretched through the fence it reached out to me.

"I'm sorry," I whispered to it, pulling the trigger and... missed. Taking another breath, I moved forward a few more steps and pulled the trigger again. This time the bullet hit it, but in the neck, a dark mess of liquid oozes from the wound. The zombie staggered back a step but immediately came at me again, its movements more frantic, both arms reaching out and walking at the fence as if trying to walk through it.

Another two steps forward, I lined up the shot again, this time aiming a little higher and stroked the trigger. The bullet hit and found the right place. Straight through the head just above the right eye, my aim was still a little off, I would have to start asking for extra lessons with the guards.

The zombie seemed to hover for a few seconds before falling backwards, landing with a satisfying thud.

"Nice shot G," lost in thought I was startled, Adam was stood behind me, there were other people, civilians and guards running towards us, worried looks on their faces, each of them carried a weapon after hearing my shot.

"Uh sorry guys, there is no threat. I was just blowing off steam." I told them sheepishly rubbing at the back of my neck.

Some mumbled, angry responses met me from the crowd,

others gave me sad, pitying looks. I honestly didn't know which was worse.

"Come on G, let's go get some food." Adam clapped his hand on my shoulder and flashed me his goofy smile.

"Sounds good," I let him lead me towards the canteen.

CHAPTER THREE

After food, which consisted of a watery chicken stew, I strolled back to the hospital area alone. Adam had gone to spend some time with Amelia over at the quarantined area. I paused to watch the sun go down, casting a beautiful orange glow over the sky. The nurse showed me to the room where Nia was being held in quarantine. Will was still there, sitting dutifully outside of the window to her room. Nia was sleeping again and the nurse would only let one of us stay, so as not to disturb her. Will informed me that the operation went well and now it was just a waiting game to see if she had an infection; zombie or otherwise. He sent me back to my room to get some rest. I didn't argue, he had more right to be there than me, plus I did feel seriously drained, my legs felt like lead weights and my head felt too heavy for my neck.

I walked back slowly, dragging my feet across the dusty ground. I closed the door to my room tightly behind me, then lay on my bed fully clothed. I closed my eyes.

It still didn't seem real, Kelly and the kids...gone. I felt the warm tears leak down my face, hot, searing pain tore through me, my stomach cramped and my chest tightened. My throat constricted and I couldn't breathe. I curled up in a ball facing the wall and just let the sobs come out.

I cried for what felt like hours, until the tears dried up and my chest and ribs ached. I got under the blankets, feeling a little better, like the blanket was some sort of a shield.

I fell asleep not long after, emotionally drained. However, nightmares plagued my rest and I didn't get a goodnight sleep after all. Tossing and turning, feeling cold because I'd kicked the blankets off me.

I woke up early, the sun was barely up but my stomach was shouting at me; empty from days of no food and a liquid diet. I made my way along the corridor, I paused by the bedroom doors of Adam and Will. Only snores met me, I left them sleeping. Our group had been through so much in the last few weeks alone that they deserved every minute of peace that they could get.

I followed my nose and the growl of my stomach to the communal food hall which was already bustling with activity. Fresh eggs on the menu today, from the chickens they kept around back. They looked good, I had my helping along with a fresh slice of doughy bread, and black coffee. I piled the eggs on top of the bread and devoured it within minutes. It was good, could have used a little butter but otherwise it was amazing. Who knows when the ingredients for the bread would run out, or when the chickens would stop laying? It was only a small spoonful of egg but I made the most of it.

I sipped at my hot, black coffee, hoping to see one of the boys come in, but none of them had made an appearance before I had finished my cup. I scooped up my plate and cup and handed it back to the lady behind the second counter, ready to be washed for the next lot of hungry diners. Thanking her with a smile and a nod of my head; it was too loud to use words.

First port of call was obviously the hospital, I jogged over. My head felt a little clearer after food and coffee. Kelly and the kids were in my thoughts, my chest still hurt. Truth be told I'd rather be just lying in bed, sleeping the days away until the military needed me. But I owed it to my family to stay alive, and live a little. For now anyway, I wanted to take out the rest of the crew and then I wanted to join my beautiful Kelly and kids in heaven.

I waved to nurse Amy as I entered through the factory doors. She smiled and gestured that I follow her.

I did, to the end of the corridor and peeked inside the room she had stopped outside of. It seemed that Nia had been moved from quarantine early.

The factory we were in used to be a battery manufacturer and already had two nurse's rooms and a human resources office in this area. Where they used to test the workers blood samples. The military had adapted one of them into an operating theatre and the HR office for a patient room. It was the last door on the right and was quite large. Eight beds occupied the room, four on each side. Seven of them unoccupied, each made meticulously with white sheets covered with what looked like an itchy grey blanket. Like the ones we had in our rooms.

I was only concerned with Nia, she looked tiny laying in the bed. She was covered up to her chest and seemed to be sleeping. The doctor was with her, checking her pulse and blood pressure.

The nurse padded quietly up to the doctor and whispered in her ear, she nodded slightly and held up two fingers, gesturing for me to join them. I took a deep breath in relief, although my heart still pounded in anticipation as to what she was going to say. I heard shuffling behind me and saw Will and then Billy.

"How is she doc?" Will asked quietly before I could.

"She was incredibly lucky, it was a deep cut but she missed any major veins or arteries. I've stitched her up and gave her a tetanus shot. She will be on a small dose of antibiotics as its all we have. I want to keep her in here for a few days to rest and because it's the cleanest area we have and the risk of infection here is lower than anywhere else." She spoke quietly but confidently, maintaining eye contact the whole time. I liked that.

I nodded, that made sense. "Ok, what can we do to help?" I asked, my eyes flickering to Nia who had started to stir.

The doctor led us all outside and closed the door to the room gently, she didn't speak but instead inclined her head towards the offices. Indicating that she would like us to follow her, which of course we did.

She moved behind her desk and sat in a blue plastic chair. "Hi all, you know that I'm Doctor Wells. I know that you all want to visit her but I'll need you to go in just one at a time. We don't want to overwhelm her ok? Also, don't forget that she is still under quarantine. Only the three of you will be permitted to enter and there will be a lock code on the door that only myself and my nurses know. Is that understood?" she gave each of us a pointed look.

We three, nodded in return, we would have agreed to anything just to see her for even five minutes.

"Billy? If you'd like to go in first," he smiled apologetically to myself and Will but disappeared through the door quickly.

"Now, you two. The reason I let Billy go first is because I have a request..." she trailed off, waiting for us to reply.

I looked at Will who raised his eyebrows; he didn't know what was coming next either.

"Ok," I nodded at her to carry on, she had gotten our interest.

"Well, this injury of Nia's is going to take up a lot of our antibiotics and pain killers. We will have enough to give her a full dose but not anyone else who may need them which is why I explained earlier that I'll have to scrimp on them." She waited for us to nod our heads, indicating that we followed her so far and that we understood her predicament.

"Now I used to work at the following private lab around an

hour from here, providing it hasn't been ransacked they should have a lot of what we would need. For now, I'd say it's our best bet,"

"Have you spoken to the Captain?" Will asked

"We have spoken about it in the past, but our main priority was fortifying this compound and trying to find survivors and food. Now that we are running low we need to make this our number one priority," she looked between us both

"I'd like you both to run lead on the next mission," she leaned slightly forward in her chair, obviously eager to hear our reply.

Well this was new, a doctor giving orders regarding missions instead of the Captain.

"Uh, forgive me for asking but shouldn't the captain be giving the orders and not the doctor?" Will was thinking the same thing as me.

"Yes," she smiled and inclined her head. "But if I go to him with names of people that are willing to go out on a supply run then he may be more willing to agree to it."

I looked at Will, shaking my head from side to side, I'd been going crazy within these walls, maybe it was time for a little road trip. I nodded slowly, Will nodded back.

"Ok, and this will help Nia too?" if we were going to risk our lives for this medicine then I wanted Nia to benefit from it.

"Absolutely! It means I can give her the full dose that she needs. I've written up a list of items we will need and things that would be useful."

"Ok, talk it over with the captain and get him to contact us with the details," I confirmed.

"Will do, you can both go and see her now. Tell Billy I'd like to see him please." she beamed at us.

We didn't argue, both of us were out of there like a shot, we opened the door to the ward quietly but needn't have. Nia was sat up, eating scrambled eggs and laughing at something Billy had said.

Her face lit up even more when she saw Will and I at the door, Will practically ran at her. I held back to catch Billy as he left

"Hey George, can't wait huh?" he grinned

"Nope I need to see her to believe that she is ok. Bill, the doctor would like to see you in her office,"

His face dropped like I hit him in the gut. "No, nothing bad, just a request," I smiled, the look of relief on his face was comical.

"Phew, you had me worried there. I'll head straight to her now." He clapped me on the shoulder and walked towards the docs' office.

I turned back towards Nia and Will who was now sat on the bed beside her. I watched them for a few moments. Will was trying to steal some of Nia's eggs 'just to try' but she wasn't having any of it and kept slapping his hand away.

"Will you two behave," I said in mock frustration

"He started it" Nia complained and poked her tongue out at Will.

"How are you?" I walked around the other side of her bed and sat in the chair provided for visitors.

"My leg feels sore and a little itchy, from the stiches I guess. The doctor said that I have to stay in for another few days?" she already looked fed up.

"Yeah, it's just a precaution, at the moment this is one of the cleanest rooms on the compound and we need to make sure you don't get an infection." Will explained.

Nia nodded but still didn't look happy. Her face looked a little pale in comparison to her dark locks which were piled high on top of her head.

"Thanks for saving me, I remember trying to get the zombies to follow me away from the other workers, then I got trapped in that office, cutting my leg on the way in there. I thought I was a goner, but I heard George's voice and saw you both outside of the room. I knew that I would be ok," her voice broke and she sounded close to tears.

"We will always be there to look out for you, but next time, don't be the hero ok?" Will kissed her in the forehead.

"Ok, but I'm soooooo bored already, please help me," she moaned.

I chuckled "I'll see if I can find some books for you to read,"

"That would be great thanks, what would be even better is a Burger with fries and a shake and a DVD night." She laughed when both Will and I groaned out loud. I missed fast food.

"That would be amazing but sadly we are fresh out of those. How about some military grade dried food pouches and whatever books I can find children's or otherwise?" I offered, winking at her.

"Perfect," she grinned back.

We heard the beeping of someone entering the door lock code and the small creak of it opening. I looked up to see the doctor gesturing that I should go to her.

"I have to go and leave you in Will's capable hands. I'll try to track down the very best books for you Madame. I'll be back later as soon as the doc ok's it," I kissed her temple and for a moment just breathed in her scent. I'd come so close to losing her and that couldn't happen again. From now on, no more alcohol and I'd go on as many supply runs as possible to ensure that my friends and what I now called my family got the best that this world still had to offer.

"What's up doc?" shit I missed bugs bunny too, my inner voice chirped up.

The doctor smiled thinly, I'd bet she'd heard that a thousand times before.

"The Captain would like to see you and Will immediately,"

"Ok no problem, just let Will in there a little longer. They both need it. I'll go and see the captain and update Will later, I'm able to speak for both of us." I felt confident that Will would be ok with me speaking on his behalf.

"Ok, thank you. Here's a list of what we need, the smaller list below the line I've drawn are things that can come in handy. You know, the reason I asked you and Will first was because I felt that you both have good motive to go and get these meds,"

I nodded, she was correct. We would protect our friends by doing anything that we could. I looked at the list, I knew what most of the things on it were.

"I'll head over and see the Captain straight away."

I exited the medical wing back out into the beautiful sunshine and headed towards the main building.

CHAPTER FOUR

It seemed quieter in the compound today and as I rounded the corner towards the main part of the building I could see why.

There were dozens of workers over at the sister compound, making a stronger fence and the foundations for the walkway between the two buildings. Just like Will and I had discussed with the Lt. yesterday. They now had armed guards watching out for them. A little too late but then we were all still learning.

I opened the door to the captains' reception; he had taken over the manager's office. The stifling heat hit me straight away, long gone were the days when we had nice cool air conditioning.

"The captain said he wanted to see me?" I smiled at the receptionist behind the desk, I'd seen her once or twice. She had come to the send-off for my family. She wore a thin navy cotton dress and flat black shoes. Her dirty blonde hair was tied up neatly in a bun with a few wisps of hair around her face. Thin black framed glasses made her pale blue eyes seem larger. Her name was Rachel, I thought to myself. I wasn't sure if she had been working with the captain before the apocalypse but she seemed extremely efficient at her job here and now.

"I'll go and see if he's ready for you George," she smiled and entered the captain's office with a small knock at the door. `

A few moments later she returned "Please go in, can I get you anything?"

"Perhaps some water please?" my throat was starting to get dry. It wasn't this hot in the hospital.

"Ah George, thanks for coming so quickly," the captain stood and extended his hand. I shook it and sat opposite him in the chair he gestured to.

"No problem Captain, how can I help you?"

There was a small knock at the door and Rachel entered carrying a tray, with a jug of water and two glasses on it. I could see the condensation running down the outside of the jug, meaning that the water was cold. I looked forward to tasting it.

She placed the tray on the table and poured water into each glass handing one to myself and one to the captain, with minimal sound.

"Thank you, Rochelle," the captain smiled.

Ah so it was Rochelle not Rachel, I'd have to remember it for next time.

I took a long drink "Yes, thank you, that's very nice. It's so hot in here compared to the hospital."

Rochelle left the room and closed the door tightly behind her.

"Yes, so far we have managed to keep the air conditioning running in the medical area although it's on very low and only for an hour or so per day."

"Ah, that explains it, well you know where to find me when it gets really hot then," I joked.

"Indeed, we shall both be sat in the waiting area," he laughed. His friendly manner mixed with his air of confidence and the authority that exuded from him demanded respect and I found that I liked him a lot. More than that I trusted him, and that went a long way in this world.

"Now, for the reason that I called for you. The doctor has sent a message that you and Will have agreed to lead a team to the facility where she used to work to see if there are still medicines and equipment there?"

"Yes, anything that will help Nia and the rest of our fellow survivors," I agreed, putting Nia's name before the others to let him know that she was the main reason that we had agreed to go.

"Let me be straight with you George, I don't like this mission one bit, its why I keep putting it off. The center you'd be headed to is here," he pointed to an area on his map.

"Now we have come as far as here and here and encountered road blocks both ways. We felt that maybe it was an ambush so we turned around and came back." He pointed at another two roads, I studied the map.

"How about this way?" I asked pointing at a backroad.

"It's a possibility but unknown territory to us, I can only spare, two maybe three men. Medicine is highly important to us but my men are spread thin as it is. A team went out three days ago and haven't returned from what should have been a few hours recon mission at the most. I need the rest of my men to make sure that the compound is secure for the civilians we have here. Where is Will?"

"Ok, I know of a few men that will accompany us also, if you could spare two men I'll take a six-man team?" I was thinking, myself, Will, Adam and Billy. "Will is still in the hospital with Nia, she was hurt in the attack yesterday."

"As long as you're sure and Will is happy with the plan, you leave first thing in the morning, lets meet back here at 1900 hours with your team, and we can go over the mission and the route."

"Ok I'll go and talk to the men now."

"Thank you, George," he nodded and began looking

through the maps again. I guessed that it was my way of being dismissed.

I walked from the Captains office, giving Rochelle a little wave as I passed. She smiled back and trotted into the captain's office. I was feeling a little more positive. I needed time outside of these walls and fences and really wanted to kick some undead ass. Plus, it felt good to be useful. I knew that Will and Billy would probably still be around the hospital area, and I had a good idea where to find Adam.

I walked around the outside of the compound towards the back and where the quarantine areas were. Taking the long way. In truth, the captain's office was a short distance from the quarantine area. But I needed a breath of fresh air after being in that stuffy office. The quarantine rooms were no more than the rest of the offices in the warehouse. Currently there were five areas that were safe enough but also comfy enough for the people suspected to be infected. Each room had a bed and a portable toilet.

As I entered the large doors I saw movement on my left. John was there with another military guy that I didn't recognise, working on a jeep.

"Hey John, how's things?" I smiled, it was nice to see a familiar face.

"Aww George, it's so good to see you. I'm sorry about... well you know," he looked awkwardly to the floor. I knew he meant well.

"I know, and thank you. Have you seen Adam?"

"Yeah, he's with Amelia." His face lit up, "He's not left her,"

I chuckled "Ah young love huh?" I joked and walked towards the direction that John had pointed. I tried to fight the pain in my chest, telling me that I'd never again get to visit Kelly anywhere but her grave.

I focused on Adam who I could now see was sat outside of the room where Amelia was being kept. He was talking to her through the small holes that had been placed in the window. She had only hours left until she was released with the all clear.

He turned as I approached him, I gave Amelia a small wave which she returned.

"Hey George, how are you man? How's Nia?" Adam got up and clapped me on the shoulder.

"Good morning both, Nia is good. Needs to stay in a little longer to make sure she heals properly, but is otherwise good."

"That's good." Amelia smiled, happy that her friend was on the mend.

"You look good Amelia, no sudden urges to eat brains?" I chirped.

"Wouldn't know, I've not seen anyone today that has any," she smiled and poked her tongue out at me.

"Touché" I replied laughing.

"So, Adam, I have a mission and I was wondering if you'd like to come with me?" turning to him.

"When do we leave?" he grinned at me.

We had been through a lot together in the short time we had known each other and had become close. He knew that I wouldn't steer him wrong. He also knew that if I was asking for help then I really needed it. Amelia on the other hand didn't know me so well and was worried about her lover.

"What's the mission? Who else is going? How safe is it?" she fired off the questions quicker than I could reply. Her good nature from the moment before had disappeared. I waited for her to finish before even trying to answer.

Adam met my eyes and raised his eyebrows, he was curious too. I couldn't blame him. I loved and trusted these men like my brothers but I wouldn't blindly enter a mission. It was always good to brainstorm with the others as we all saw things differently and each had great ideas.

"Ok the mission is to travel to a medical Center about an hour away, get some anti biotics and other medicines, then come back. A simple supply run. I'm going, I'm hoping that Adam, Will and Billy will accompany me along with two of the captain's men. As to how safe it is, well it's the end of the world, nothing is ever safe, but I can assure you that I will have his back as I know he will have mine."

She seemed satisfied with my answer but still not happy. Knowing that my word was as good as it would get. Nothing was ever guaranteed anymore.

"Ok then, the captain wants us to meet in his office tonight at 7. Hope to see you there Adam. Amelia hope you get out of there soon," I smiled at both warmly, even if Adam decided not to come, I would never hold it against him. I knew that they would need to talk about it, they were a couple now, Adam could no longer make decisions like this alone.

"One hour and forty minutes and counting." She smiled back. "See you later George."

I turned and walked away, cringing when I heard their loudly whispered argument from behind me. Wow was I going to be unpopular.

Next stop was the hospital wing. I washed my hands at the nurse's station before entering the ward, after the nurse had entered the door code.

Will was sat with Nia, he was reading to her, her eyes were closed but she had a smile on her face. When they heard the squeak of the door opening they both looked at me.

"I'm sorry, were you resting?" I smiled apologetically and stopped half in the room and half out in case they wanted me to leave.

"No, just listening to uncle Will reading. He used to do it for me when I was little." A little of her color was coming back and she looked a lot better even in the short time that I was gone.

"Why Will, I didn't know you could read?" I teased

"Cheeky," he returned, throwing the book at me, missing and falling just short at my feet.

I picked up the book and threw it back at him, then nodded with my head that he should join me out in the corridor.

"I'll be back in a moment love." Will placed the book on the bed by the side of her.

"All ok?" she looked at me worried.

"Yeah all is good, just updating Will on tomorrows duties. Amelia says hi, I'm sure that once she's been cleared that she will come to see you." I tried to sound re assuring.

"Mmmm well ok then. See you later George," she gave me a suspicious look to which I stuck my tongue out. Nia rolled her eyes and laughed before picking up the book and reading it.

"What's up?" Will closed the door behind him fully, hearing the lock click into place.

"Let's go and find the doc so that I can tell you together." I said turning and heading towards her office.

She was sat in her small room behind her desk writing in a yellow legal notepad.

"Hey Doc, I've spoken to the captain. He wants us all to meet in his office tonight at 7. Just to go over the final details, I'd appreciate it if you could join us."

"Yes of course, that's excellent news. Thank you both, I really appreciate it." She beamed at us.

"Will are you still in? I'd like to take a team of six."

"Yeah of course I'm still in. Adam and Billy?" Will replied.

The other two men were just obvious choices. We knew them well and knew that we could trust them.

"I hope so yeah, if Amelia let's Adam." I winked letting them know that I was joking, well kind of.

"Ok that's excellent. I cannot tell you how excited I am to be getting the meds that we need. I don't suppose that there's any chance of me tagging along?" she looked really hopeful, I wasn't sure if she was just as stir crazy here as me or if it was because she wanted to see something from a life long gone.

"You'd have to ask the captain, to be honest I think that you would be needed more here than with us. We have the list you gave us and any plans and info that you have on the facility would be extremely useful," I smiled at her not wanting her to think that I didn't want her to come.

Truth was I didn't want her on the supply run with us. She was just another person that we would have to protect, her knowledge of the facility would come in handy but she could also get in the way and get harmed. Anything could happen on these runs. I didn't want to make the call that could see our camp without a doctor.

"Ok I shall come to the meeting later and perhaps you are correct. I probably am of more use if I stay here. I'll write down all I can remember about the facility, here take my key card, it will grant you access to most of the rooms there." She handed the key card to me, her hand felt cold against mine, it caused me to shudder.

"Sorry, it's the air con," she said by way of explanation.

"You're lucky you have it, wait until you get to the captain's office later." I laughed.

"I'll bet. Right, I'll go and check on Nia's dressing now and maybe give her a new one. You two go get some dinner or take a walk ok? Give her a few hours rest." The doctor advised using her no-nonsense voice. She sounded quite stern when she wanted to.

"Just don't tell her about the run ok doc?" Will begged giving his best puppy dog look.

"No problem, I'm the one wanting her to get rest and not be worried. She didn't sleep particularly well last night, I'll be giving her a sedative this evening around 8. So, I'll need all visitors gone by then. It should knock her out for a good twelve hours."

"Ok, sounds good, tell her I'll come back later. See you later doc."

"Bye Will." she smiled at him and I swear she batted her eyelashes.

"Bye doc." I grinned

"Uh yes, bye George," she cleared her throat and looked away quickly but not before I saw the scarlet shade of her cheeks.

Will and I left the office and walked towards the canteen.

"What are you grinning about?" Will asked

"That doctor wants you." I wiggled my eyebrows

"Wants me to do what?" he asked looking totally confused.

"You know, she wants you, she wants your body," I sang in a mocking tone.

"Shut up, no, she... Really?"

"Yeah man, how can you not see the way that she looks at you?"

"I guess I never really noticed. Huh, she is kinda cute," he looked really pleased about it. I chuckled but remained silent and left him to his thoughts.

We entered the canteen and joined Billy at a table close to the main doors, he was just finishing up his food.

"What's for lunch today?" Will asked clapping him on the back.

"Hey guys, its pasta with a watery white sauce. It's really good though." he answered with his mouthful.

I carried on walking to the serving hatch to get my bowl, it did look and smell delicious. Will was close on my heels, probably just as ravenous as I was.

I saw a familiar face in the kitchen, Kandace smiled at us and came to serve Will and me.

"Hey boys, how are you both," her eyes flickered to me, then to Will. Another person feeling bad for me.

"I'm ok thanks, all things considered." I answered honestly.

"That's great George. How's Nia?" she scooped up the pasta and put it into a white bowl with little pink flowers over it.

"She's getting better but doc wants her to stay in a few more days." Will replied grabbing my bowl of food as I was too slow.

"Hey," I complained

"Too slow, sorry not sorry," Will laughed ducking out of my way and back to the table. I shook my head and chuckled.

"The cheek!" Kandace said smiling, she placed an extra scoop into my bowl and winked at me.

"See you later George."

"You too sweetheart, thank you." I held my bowl in salute and walked back to the table.

Billy had gotten us a jug of water and three white mugs and placed it in the middle of the table.

"I was just filling Billy in on the doc's mission for us," Will informed me, in between huge forkfuls of food that he was shoving into his mouth like he hadn't eaten in weeks. But then again, we hadn't eaten properly in months, since we had to ration everything.

"What do you think? Are you in?" I took a bite of my own, the creamy richness was so good. A little watery but it didn't take away from the flavor.

"Yeah, the captain has already asked me to join you." Billy smiled, he had just eaten the last of his food and took a sip of water.

"That's great thank you. It's nice to know we will have a few men there that will watch our backs."

"Captain Coopers men are our men now and they will protect you and the other members of this compound above all others." Billy sounded so serious, that at first, I thought that he was being sarcastic. But one look at his face told me that he fully believed what he was saying.

Will looked at me with his eyes wide. A 'what the hell was that' kinda look.

"I'm sure they will," I nodded. I fully believed that they would protect us for as long as they could. However, I wasn't sure how many of them had been through what Will and his men had, had Captain Cooper's men ever had a near miss? I wasn't so sure about how things would go down if we were backed into a corner, I'd like to think that they would help us out but sometimes when it came down to it, some people were 'every man for themselves'.

Billy nodded seeming satisfied with my response. "I've decided to join the military, they need all the men that they can get now plus this would give me the extra training and fitness that I need to survive in this harsh new world." He told us proudly, puffing out his chest.

The last bit seemed as though he was reading from a script, maybe they were the Lieutenants words and not Billy's. Didn't matter though because what he was saying was correct. Those skills would help him to survive should anything happen to this place.

Billy had given me an idea. He and Will started to talk about Nia and her health. I finished my food and collected the three bowls, taking them back to the hatch. Kandace was no longer in sight, so I thanked the tall thin woman who had now taken over.

Instead of going back to the table I made my way to the notice board, there were many things on there. Weapons training times, available jobs, missing people posters could be put on the board at the back of the room now as this one was getting too full.

I made a note of the survival training days and times. I wanted to be able to care for myself and my friends should we ever find ourselves alone in the world again.

Survival training was a mixture of little skills. Building camp fires, how to build a shelter out of items you can find outside, a little weapons training and more. I'd see the captain and see if a few of us could attend the next session.

"George I'm headed out, I have rounds. I'll meet up with you all later." Billy called out. I gave a small wave and retraced my steps back to the table.

"You headed back to see Nia?" I asked Will, already knowing what the answer would be.

"Yeah, I'm going to have a shower first," he leaned back in his chair, yawned and gave a huge stretch. He had dark circles under his eyes.

This last week had taken a lot out of all of us. I knew that Will and Adam felt the loss of my family deeply. I should talk to them and thank them for being there and for taking care of... well for doing what needed to be done. I just wasn't ready.

I nodded, we were allowed to use the showers but sparingly. The water was only luke warm but it was soooo good.

"Ok, I have a few things I need to get done also." I didn't tell him about the training sessions, I'm sure he already knew but I wanted to ask the Captain if he could fit us in first.

I left the canteen just after him and headed to the rooms they were currently using for classrooms. Until the other compound was ready, the schooling area was located in the corridor adjacent to the canteen.

I arrived in the corridor quickly and followed the joyful sound of children's laughter.

CHAPTER FIVE

I stood outside the first room that I came to. The door to the classroom was closed. I watched the teacher talk to the children through the glass window in the top of the door. I couldn't hear what he said to them but the little people seemed to love it. It tugged at my heart strings to watch their little faces light up at something their teacher had said.

I began to get all choked up, before I started crying again I knocked at the door. The teacher came to the door "Can I help you?" his voice was deep but remarkably gentle.

He had chocolate brown skin and his eyes were Jade. His jet-black hair was shaved closely to his head and he had on a pair of combat trousers and navy t shirt. He wore a guarded expression on his face. After all, it was his job to protect our future generation and he didn't know me.

"Yeah, I was looking for the library room, please?" my eyes flickered to the curious little faces back in the room.

"Oh, its two doors down on the left," he pointed down the corridor. I nodded my thanks and started to walk that way, I heard the classroom door close, once again leaving me alone.

The library room was no more than a few shelves of tattered

books that people had brought from home with them or that the soldiers had found. Books were not a high priority but they would come in handy for the children.

I had a good look through the paperbacks and chose a few books of different genres that I thought Nia may like, anything to help her with her boredom. It might convince her to stay a little while longer in the hospital wing if she had something to distract her.

I signed out the books on a little pad that had been left there and exited the room, closing the door softly behind me.

I could hear loud excited voices from the classroom opposite the library and peeked in. These were older children, I'd say from the ages of 10-13. At the age of 14 the captain felt that they were old enough to train with the adults.

The teacher had them doing fitness in this classroom, they were playing some sort of indoor obstacle course. All of the tables and chairs had been stacked neatly around the walls of the room giving them plenty of space to run and jump about.

I laughed at the teacher showing them how to do it and pretending to be clumsy, to take off any apprehension some of the smaller ones may have had.

She saw me watching her and waved, her red cheeks giving away that she was embarrassed at being caught playing the fool. I turned away not wanting to distract her further and it was then that I saw the notice board, they were asking for any books people may still have and advertising for a classroom assistant/librarian.

I left slowly, heading back towards the hospital wing. Excited to tell Nia about the new job opportunity that would be perfect for her. She was kind and caring but could be super strict and kind of scary when she needed to be. Good traits for a teacher and/or librarian. However, I also had in mind what the doctor had said about Nia getting some rest, so I took the scenic route, around the exterior of the buildings. I paused to watch the construction of the new fences over at compound two, after the last attack they were wasting no time and it already looked a lot more secure than before. They had inserted large metal spikes that ran from the fence panels and into the ground in the hopes it would make the fence more secure.

It was a little busier in the medical area this time. Nurse Amy was accompanied by another man and woman, not dressed in medical gear but dressed smartly in trousers and shirts. They were taking instructions off Amy and looking closely at a dummy person.

"What did that dummy ever do to you?" I chirped.

"Why? You offering to take its place?" Amy asked.

I got closer and could see a rubber band around its arm and a needle poking out of it.

I could feel myself getting paler "Uh, no thanks, I'll stick to just visiting." I gave her a small grin, feeling slightly squeamish.

"Chicken," she teased and inclined her head that I should follow her.

I grinned at the two students and got a chuckle out of them before following Nurse Amy.

She entered the code to the ward and for once when I entered the room, Nia was alone. She had changed into a bright orange vest top and grey shorts. It was a little warmer in here now but still not as hot as the captain's office was earlier on.

"Hey George," Nia smiled, placing down the book that she had been reading. The cover was missing off it and so I wasn't sure what it was but she seemed to be enjoying it.

"Hey sweetheart, I've brought you some more books, but I wasn't sure what ones you would like." I handed her the pile of paperbacks.

She looked through them, I noticed that when she stacked them onto her side table she added the horror ones on top.

"So, you like the scary ones huh?" I grinned and nodded towards the stack.

"Yeah, love a good murder mystery too. What did you think I'd like?"

"Uh, those girly gooey romance books with the hot hunks and steamy scenes." I wiggled my eyebrows up and down.

"Oh, don't worry, I've got my very own real-life hunks right here." she winked.

"I can take those others back if you want?"

"Nah that's ok, I'll give them a go. Thank you for bringing them. I'm so bored here. Tell me what you've been up to?" she settled back into her array of different cushions which had been propped up behind her and I got comfortable in the chair.

I filled her in on what I had been up to and what was for dinner, she said that she had already had her dinner and got extra helpings. I explained about the job boards and the available teaching assistant/librarian opening. Her eyes sparkled when I told her and she said that she would speak to the captain as soon as possible.

This made me happy and I knew that Will would be over the moon also. The job would be much safer for her than securing and cleaning out the second compound. Plus, as a teacher she was less likely to be called on for sentry duty or supply missions.

"I'll be seeing the captain later, I shall let him know of your interest in the position," she clapped her hands together excitedly and did a little dance. Before she took in a sharp breath and her face creased in pain.

"Are you ok?" I stood up and moved to her side.

"Yeah I'm good. They have had to cut back on pain killers as we are running out."

"That's not good, you need them." I was worried about her, tomorrow couldn't come quick enough. I would make sure that we got everything we could off the list.

"It's ok, I just caught it in the sheets as I was doing my happy dance," she smiled up at me.

"As long as you're sure?" I sat back down, still concerned but knowing that until we got the extra medication there wasn't any more that I could do for her.

"Yeah, I'm good really, I promise to say in the hospital until the doctor clears me. Oh, and George could you do me a favor?"

"Yeah, anything," I meant it

"When you go on the supply run could you please look for some art supplies?" she smiled widely and batted her eyelashes.

"What supply run? I don't know~" I tried to play dumb but she cut me off.

"Cut the crap George, I know that you and Will are planning something. Billy stopped by," she faked anger.

Shit, that bloody Billy, he couldn't keep a secret from her.

I looked to the floor, embarrassed at being caught out.

"So?" she demanded

"So, what?"

"What are you up to?"

"It's just a simple supply run, drive there, get the stuff, and come back." I shrugged my shoulders trying to make it sound easy, avoiding her eyes.

"George, we both know that in this world there is no such thing as simple. Sometimes the things you need maybe the closest to you or the furthest thing away. With multiple enemies waiting to hurt you."

I wasn't sure if we were still talking about the supply run or something else. I was too chicken to ask.

"Yeah, well I promise that I will protect both Will and Billy, we also have Adam coming with us and a couple of the captains men. We are only driving twenty minutes away."

"Ok then. But please be safe."

"I will." I lifted her hand and kissed it"

"George, I-"

We were interrupted by the doctor "Good afternoon both.

Nia I've just come to top up your pain killers and your anti biotics. You've eaten your lunch, right?" Dr. Wells asked.

"Yep, all gone." Nia smiled, the doctor handed her three tablets.

"A good appetite is a must have when you're healing. So is rest." Doctor Annabelle looked straight at me.

I smiled and tried to bat my eyelashes at her. It worked for Nia, why not for me?

"Doesn't work George." Annabelle said but she did laugh and shake her head.

The doc left and I could see the tablets were taking the edge off the pain but only for a short while as they were not strong enough. They did however make her sleepy and allowed her to get more rest that she normally would.

We spoke a little bit more about the types of art supplies that she wanted and how she had always loved art. She also thought that the children would love it. I had to agree with that, in my experience there was nothing that children liked more than to get their little hands messy.

"I'll see you later sweetheart ok?" I smiled fondly, as she yawned loudly.

"Please don't go on the run before saying goodbye, Will, Adam and Billy too please."

"We will stop by tonight and in the morning, I promise. As long as you promise to get some rest." I kissed her head and left, after she pinky swore to sleep some.

It was strange that Will had not stopped by the hospital to visit Nia. I started in the direction of our living quarters when I bumped into a large, solid body running around the corner.

We both went over with him landing on top of me, forcing the air from my lungs and winding me.

"Ooomph,"

"Ah hell sorry." Will apologised.

He rolled off me, got up and extended his hand to help me

up, which I gratefully took. I bent over at the waist trying to catch my breath. I tried to put my weight on my right ankle and a sharp pain shot up my leg.

"You ok man?"

"Yeah...just...winded," I huffed out.

He led me over to a small wall and sat me down, sitting next to me.

"I'm sorry, I had a wash then lay on the bed and fell asleep. I woke up and realised that I was late to visit Nia. I ran straight here and I guess I wasn't looking where I was going,"

"That's ok... she's just...gone to... sleep." my breathing was getting easier.

"Damn it." he sounded so sad that I immediately wanted to make him feel better.

"I was with her though, took her some books."

"Thank you, G, since she is sleeping. Fancy going to the main gardens, they are doing a class on first aid?" he asked. We still hadn't been given jobs and this would be a useful skill to learn. I'd done it years ago when Poppy was born but had never brushed up on it.

"Sounds good." I tried to stand up and the pain crippled me. "Ah" I sucked in air through gritted teeth.

"What's wrong?" Will looked at me concerned.

"I think I've twisted my ankle."

"That's not good, come on let's go to see Anna- I mean Dr. Wells," I put my arm around his shoulders and he supported my weight.

"Oh yes let's go see *Annabelle,*" I mocked.

"Shut up G." he said, he tried to look stern but I could see the hint of a smile around the corners of his mouth and definitely in his eyes.

I was happy that he liked her too and hoped that they could make a go of it or at least keep each other happy for a short while in this dead world.

It took us a while to get back to the hospital wing with me limping along and Will dragging me, I wasn't exactly small or light.

The doctor, who was sat at the nurse's station with the man from earlier, jumped up as we hobbled in "What happened?" she frowned.

"We bumped into each other, and this big lump landed on top of me. I think it's twisted." I tried not to moan but it hurt terrible, I'd always had a good pain threshold and it caused me to worry that I'd broken something.

"Come into the ward and get him up onto a bed."

She entered the code for the ward and ushered us in, placing a finger to her lips to ask us to be quiet.

Will helped me forward and hoisted me up onto the bed opposite Nia who was fast asleep.

I tried hard not to call out loud when my ankle banged against the metal frame of the bed. I clamped my lips together so that the sound was like a strangled cry.

"Careful," the doctor admonished Will.

I laid back, closed my eyes, and tried to think of other things as the doctor pulled off my boot. She started to prod at my ankle, pressing her fingers into my tender flesh.

I tensed up and held my breath, each time she poked my ankle it sent sparks of hot pain searing through it.

"It's severely swollen, I can't feel a break. I think that it's just badly sprained, but I can't be sure. What I do know, is that you will have to keep off this leg for at least 48 hours. I may be able to tell you more when the swelling goes down."

"Doc, I have the supply run tomorrow," I tried to get up, but she pushed me back down; she was surprisingly strong for her small size.

"It hurts me to say it George, but you're not going anywhere on that foot. For the next 48 to 72 hours you are going to lie in this bed with your foot elevated, I'll get you some cold packs to go on it and a support which will help to compress the wound and stop the swelling."

She turned and walked back through the door before I could argue any more. It was pointless anyway, I was no good to the men like this, I would only hinder them.

"I'm sorry George." Will looked genuinely upset, the corners of his mouth were turned down. I could see the worry in his eyes.

"Hey, it was an accident. I'm sorry I can't come with you tomorrow. Want to ask if we can wait a few days?" I asked hoping that he would say yes. I was so looking forward to getting out of here for a few hours. Plus, we had become a team; it didn't feel right them leaving without me.

"Nah its ok, it's just a simple run, right? I'll ask one of the other men to come with me." He smiled and checked his watch.

We chatted for a while longer about my visit with Nia and the job boards.

"It all sounds good, better to be safe than sorry and get the skills we need to survive, you never know what tomorrow will bring." Was his response when I told him about the training sessions.

"I'd better go and round up the other guys to meet in the captain's office. I'll check back in later." He left quickly too, I think he was still feeling guilty for putting me in here.

I looked across to Nia, she had slept through it all. She looked so peaceful.

The door opened again, the doctor entered, followed by Amy.

"George this is Nurse May, she will look after you when I'm not around." She nodded to the nurse standing on my left.

"Please take these," the nurse held out two tablets for me and then a white plastic glass of water.

"No thanks,"

She looked at the doctor, unsure on what she should do.

"George, you'll need the pain meds, they will help you to get comfortable and get the rest that you will need tonight."

"Nope, keep them for Nia." I shook my head, I would rather Nia get them, she was in hell of a lot more pain than I was. I would get by just fine.

"I'm sure she will appreciate the offer. How about we do a deal?" the doctor had a glint in her eye.

"I'm listening," I looked back at her suspiciously. My eyes flickered to the nurse who was watching our exchange with interest.

"How about you take these two, just for you to get a good rest tonight and I'll see that Nia gets your ration of tablets tomorrow afternoon? She already gets her own in the morning and night." The doctor offered.

If I could help Nia to feel better and to heal quicker then I would "Ok then, sounds good to me," I nodded, the doctor smiled like the cat who got the cream. I had a feeling that she was used to getting her way.

I thanked the nurse and took the two tablets off her, popping the both tablets at once and washing them down with the water that she held out to me.

I swore under my breath and blushed as the doctor raised her eyebrows at me. "Sorry doc, that hurts," she was putting on the stretchy white bandage and placing my leg in a stirrup to keep it elevated.

"Make sure to let either myself or Nurse May know if you need anything. We also have two trainees here called Ben and Nara who will check on you both in the nights."

I nodded, "Ok thanks." I pulled the blanket up over me as best I could. It was chilly in the ward in the evenings.

The Doctor gently woke Nia up for her check-up and tablets.

"What the hell happened to you?" Nia's eyes were wide in shock at seeing me in the bed across from her.

I explained what had happened to me as the doctor did her thing.

"I think Will just wanted to take me out of action for tomorrow so that he can get all the glory." I finished smiling widely and tried to reassure Nia that I was ok.

"Nia, do you need anything else?" The doctor asked after Nia had swallowed her pills.

"Oh yes please Doctor Wells, please, please, please make George wear a hospital gown." Nia's eyes sparkled mischievously.

"Oh, I will if he's not a good patient. I'll go and see if I have any gowns available. Then I'll check what's for dinner. Be good George." the Doctor winked at me and chuckled as she walked away.

"So, I guess were roommates again?" Nia smiled at me.

Maybe this stay wouldn't be so bad after all, I thought to myself.

CHAPTER SIX

The tablets hit me hard, I remember talking a little with Nia, but that's it. I couldn't even remember having dinner. But it was the best night's sleep that I'd had in weeks, months even. I woke up feeling a lot stronger and a lot more alert than I had done in quite a while. My ankle still throbbed but didn't hurt unless I tried to put weight on it or bumped it.

One of the staff members had left crutches by the side of my bed. I wasn't a stranger to them, I'd broken my leg on a skiing trip that Kelly and I had taken when we were first dating and was on crutches for six weeks.

Damn... Kelly. I closed my eyes, remembering how she looked on our wedding day. I was scared that my memory would fade and that one day I was going to forget how she smiled, how her hair fell, the sound of her laugh. I'd brought a photo album from home with loads of family pictures in it. It was under my bed in my room. I hadn't opened it yet, I didn't feel strong enough. Maybe one day soon.

I opened my eyes and took a deep breath. Everything was quiet, Nia was reading.

"Morning." I croaked.

"Good morning sleepy head." she grinned.

I sat up and swung my legs off the side of the bed, being careful not to hit my injured one.

I poured a glass of water and pulled my crutches towards me.

I got up slowly and made my way towards the bathroom, wobbling a little. I tested placing some weight on my foot but it was no use.

As I got closer to Nia's bed I noticed that she had an empty bowl by her bed. I'd slept through breakfast.

"What time is it?" I nodded to her bowl.

"It's around 11am maybe later."

"Wow, those meds are awesome." I stumbled into the bathroom and managed to use it without hurting myself further.

When I re-entered the ward, the doctor was in there checking on Nia's dressings.

"Ah, its healing nicely, doesn't seem to have any infection there. How does it feel?" she covered it up with a new dressing.

"Yeah, it's ok, it doesn't hurt so much anymore. It's more like an ache now."

"Yes, it was a bad cut, I'm sure that you will feel it for a while. But I'm pleased with your recovery. I'll release you tomorrow but you'll still need to rest it ok?"

"Yes!" Nia was happy that she was getting out of the hospital.

"Now George, how are you feeling today?" the doctor turned to me and walked to the side of my bed.

"I'm ok. I had a good rest." I was sitting on top of my covers still in my clothes from the day before.

"I'm glad, you need to keep that foot up as much as possible again today. Will and your other friends stopped by earlier, to see you and Nia. Will left those," she pointed to some clothes draped over the chair on my left. I don't know how I had missed them.

"That's great doc thanks." I was grateful to have something clean to change into, but sad that I had not seen Will and the others to say good luck before they left.

"Do you want some cereal? I can get someone to bring you some?"

My stomach was growling at me, before the world I used to know ended I wasn't a lover of cereal. Now I'd eat anything.

"Yes please," I yawned, wow even after all that sleep I was still tired.

She said someone would bring me some shortly, then disappeared back through the doors.

"So, did Will and the boys seem ok? Who else went with them?" I was itching to be on the road with them. I also felt a little guilty that it was a mission that I had accepted and then invited them all to go on and I was the one that stayed behind.

"They took an extra man from the captain's crew. Will said that the captain is going to start asking the other survivors to start doing runs if this one is successful."

"Sounds good, he told me that his men are running thin. I'm thinking that once I get out of here that I'll start taking classes. Survival ones."

"I'd like to as well, just the basic ones. I've thought about what you said George. I'm going to ask the captain about the assistant teacher position." She looked happy. And it made my heart grow a little.

"I think that you will be an amazing teacher, Nia, you're kind and caring. The little ones will love you," I told her honestly.

"Thank you, George. Any idea what job you will sign up for?"

I wasn't sure if I wanted to tell her, I didn't want to cause her any more worry.

"Uh... I was thinking maybe supply runs?" I looked away from her, knowing what would come next.

"George, no! are you serious! We finally have a safe place for all of us and you want to leave?" she asked sounding shocked.

"Ni, I just need to get out of here, from behind these walls. It won't be all the time. I just need to get away from... here"

"Or is it because you want to get away from me?" she sounded hurt.

"Ni, no. I care about you, Will and the others. We're good friends. You just don't get it, you never will" I shook my head at my outburst and my inability to explain what I felt cooped up in here.

I didn't want to say aloud what I truly felt in my heart. That if I'd tried harder to get back home then maybe my wife and children would be alive and here with me now. That it was all my fault the three people that I cared the most about in the world were now six feet under.

I closed my eyes and gulped, trying to hold back my own tears. Trying to keep the pain off my face.

"I..." Her mouth opened like she wanted to say something else, her eyes were full of unshed tears.

She turned on her side away from me.

"Ni-"

"Just leave it George, I get it. You can't face me anymore. I understand that much,"

"No, it's not-" I tried to explain but she cut me off

"I'm tired, I just want to sleep."

The door to the ward opened and in came a woman from the kitchen carrying a tray. She smiled widely, and came straight to my bed, placing the tray on my bedside table.

"There you go sugar. I'll be back later to collect the dishes." then she was gone.

The tray contained, a little cup of milk, a bowl of cereal and a black cup of coffee. I was so grateful that the military still had cereal and coffee. They also had access to chickens and cattle.

I pulled the tray onto my lap and used the milk for my

cereal, leaving my coffee black. It was stronger that way and I hoped that it may wake me up a little more.

I ate slowly, going over and over my conversation with Nia. She was reading way more into it than there really was. It wasn't her or the others that I was trying to get away from. It was the two freshly covered graves outside.

I cried silently into my coffee, I didn't know what else to do. I hoped that when I went on runs that the adrenaline and danger would distract me even for a little while from the horror and agony that was now my reality.

I placed my empty cup back on the tray and got off the bed, picking up the change of clothes that the boys had left for me.

I hobbled once again as quietly as I could to the bathroom, locking the door behind me. I stripped down and looked at myself in the mirror.

My body was now hard and lean after months of very little food. I would have to start working on my fitness levels. My hair had gotten a little longer and I needed a shave.

I washed using the bar of soap and a cloth that had been left on the wash basin. The water was cold but felt good.

I dried off with the rough burgundy towel hanging on the towel rail and got dressed quickly. Goosebumps covering my skin from head to toe.

Entering the room again, I looked towards Nia.

"Nia?" I saw her body tense even though she didn't reply and kept her eyes closed.

I got onto her bed behind her struggling to pull my leg up. I put my arm around her cuddling her in close. "Ni, it's not you guys that I need to get away from."

"I know," she whispered.

"Good, because I don't want to lose you too."

She turned towards me and looked into my eyes. Hers seeing right into my soul.

"You won't George. I do understand, really, I do. Just be careful when you're outside of the gates ok?"

"I will I promise," I hugged her close again and kissed her forehead.

"Can I borrow a book?" I asked

"Of course." Nia turned away from me and sat up, handing me the pile of books. I chose a horror one about a haunted house.

I got off her bed and limped back to my own, propping up my mismatched pillows to be able to sit up comfortably.

Each of us started to read and before long we were both silent; engrossed in our stories.

I jumped when the door opened, shocked that I had read almost a quarter of the book.

It was Lt. Jacks, panic hit me. "What's happened? Are the boys ok?" I was certain that he was going to inform us that the boys had gotten into trouble.

"Yes, don't worry, they checked in about half an hour ago, they were just getting to the site."

"Ok." I felt a little better but still wished that I was right beside them.

"How's the ankle?" he asked

"It's sore, I can't put any weight on it," I grumped.

He nodded "I'm sure you'll be back on your feet in no time. I've come to talk to you about the captain's new idea," he pulled out the blue plastic chair from against the wall and positioned it in a way that he could speak to both myself and Nia.

"How are you miss?" he attempted a smile at Nia, it looked more like he was in pain. I don't think he was used to smiling.

"Yeah I'm good thank you. Should get out of here today. And its Nia, please."

"That's great miss, I mean Nia."

"So, what did you want to talk with us about?" I was curious as to why the captain would send his second in command to see us.

"I've been talking to some other survivors this morning and throughout the following week will be talking to everyone individually and then as a group hopefully next week. We want to start training people on jobs. Cooking, gardening, taking care of the animals, sentry duty, etc. Our hope is that eventually this will all be run by you survivors and that we can move onto another town, to try to help other people."

"Wow, that sounds amazing," Nia exclaimed.

It did sound good, the fact that we would be part of the fight against the apocalypse, that we may make a difference.

"So, I'm here to ask you what type of work you're interested in? what you've done in the past?"

I looked at Nia pointedly

"Uh, I'd like to apply for the teaching assistant post please," she said quietly.

"Ok," he nodded, writing it onto a notepad that I hadn't even seen him carrying in.

"George?"

"I'd like to train and go on supply runs." My eyes flickered to Nia who looked down at her blanket.

"Ok, are you sure? We haven't had too many people volunteer to leave." his eyes bore into me.

"Yes, I'm sure, it's something I've thought about a lot. I think that with the proper training and support that I can help this camp to thrive."

He nodded his head, he looked happy with my reply. I was just telling the truth. Whatever time I had left in this wasteland I wanted to help as many people as I could.

"Ok, I've already asked your friends before they left this morning,"

"Oh yeah?" this had gotten Nia's attention. She sat up straighter and lifted her head.

"Yep I started with you guys, whilst another of my colleagues is doing the main survivor area."

"Why us?"

"Because you have already lived as a group, you are used to this type of communal camp, running its self. Over the next few weeks we will be holding elections for the people to vote in a council. This council will essentially be in charge although we are hoping for democracy and not a dictatorship"

"Will all you military men be leaving?" Nia looked a little scared.

"Eventually, but to start we will use this as our base of operations. We will be leaving in teams to go and look for other suitable compounds to build up for other survivors or to use as a backup base just in case..." he trailed off. He wanted to say just in case this one ever got overrun but didn't want to worry us.

"Ok this all sounds good, in theory," I was a little skeptical that it could be done. I'd seen the devastation back at Deacons place when the zombies invaded a camp like this. I assumed that here they would just keep expanding and bring people back here.

Now that I thought about it though it made sense to have multiple camps all over.

"We will get there George, we will succeed in our fight against the undead."

"Can you tell us what jobs our friends picked?" Nia enquired.

"Well so far I've only seen the men that left this morning. He checked his list. Adam and Will have chosen sentry duty, Billy has joined Captain Coopers' military, Amelia was with them his morning saying good bye. She chose gardening and kitchen duties."

"Military, Billy chose to leave us and join you, when you leave?" Nia sounded just as shocked as I felt.

"No in fact he has joined us to help this camp. You see who

ever will be on the council will have joined the military. They will receive more intense training than the rest as they will be making the final decisions on things. They will also have access to the weapons and rations. Billy will be the first member of your council, the only one not to be elected."

"Why Billy?" I was shocked that he would be the very first council member. Don't get me wrong it's not that I didn't like him but he was dreadfully young and naïve.

"I know that he's young but I think that's what we need, besides it was his idea about getting a self-sufficient camp so that the military could help elsewhere." Almost as if he'd read my mind. He stood up getting ready to leave.

"Well that's great," I couldn't think of anything else to say. It was an amazing idea. The more people that we could help the better. Plus, it would be good to know of another safe area that we could escape to should we ever run into trouble out on the road or if this place was overrun.

He nodded and left without another word.

"Well that's something exciting but scary to think about! Our own place." Nia grinned. I hoped that she would eventually accept that I needed to be on the move. Outside of these gates.

Plus, I wouldn't be out all the time. Just a few days or weeks per month.

"Definitely scary with Billy in charge." I laughed. Nia laughed too, the melodic sound brightened my day.

We talked for a while about all the possibilities that could happen as our camp continued to grow and strengthen. We had only been here a few days for me but honestly, I felt safer here than I had in weeks at the old place and I desperately wanted it to be successful. A place where we could not only survive but thrive.

The doctor came in at around 4pm dressed in purple scrubs, her hair was thrown up into a neat bun. Annabelle and Amy were the only two I had seen wearing proper medical uniform. I guessed by those two wearing the proper gear it differentiated them from the other two trainee nurses, Ben and Nara. Doctor Annabelle sent Nia back to the living quarters. Nia couldn't get out of bed quick enough, she began stuffing her clothes into a small bag.

"Will you be ok?" I asked, concerned that most of our friends had left the compound and we had yet to hear that they had returned. That despite the camp being full that she would be alone because we hadn't had a chance to meet the other survivors properly.

"Of course, I will, I can't wait to get out of here. Amelia is still here. I'll come back later to see you. Plus, the doc says I must check in each day for the next week, you'll be sick of me before long. Here, take these." She smiled and handed me the stack of books that I'd gotten for her the day before, minus the one that she had been reading.

"Why, thank you," I placed them on the foot of my bed.

"I'll never be sick of you Ni. Now go, have fun and be safe." I shooed her away with my hands.

"Will do, boss." she saluted me and let out a girly laugh. She really was happy to be free. I'll bet it was extremely boring sat in bed, alone for most of the day, and I was going to be in here for probably another two days. Oh, let the joy begin.

Nia was right it was incredibly boring in the hospital wing. I'd gotten out of bed a few hours ago and hobbled out to the nurse's station to have a talk with Amy. She seemed happy about it and chatted away nonstop about how good it was here compared to the last camp that she was in. My ears perked up a little

"There's another camp like this?" I asked, I don't know why I thought that this was the first one that the military had attempted. Probably because the Captain hadn't mentioned it during our little chat and I thought that Deacon would have brought it up. He must not have known.

"Oh yes, I'm from one up North, I trained up there. I was in my third year of health at college when this happened. Just a few months out from graduating. Anyway, they had a few nurses and doctors at the old place and so they sent myself and Annabelle here." she smiled she didn't seem disappointed, but rather quite smug that she had been chosen.

"Ah, so we are the second compound that the army have put together?" this was good news. It proved that Billy's plan had worked before. I was positive that we could also become self-sufficient.

"So, did all the army men and women leave the old camp, how does it work now?"

"No, we are the third camp I think. I'm not sure how it works there now, you'd have to ask the Captain or Lt Jacks. But I know that some of them stayed behind. Annabelle and I were amongst the first people to arrive at this camp. We brought Weapons and livestock with us, along with food clothing, water and bedding. The men go out on supply missions and bring us back what they can also. We have been here for nearly three months and I'm so proud of how it has grown."

"Wow, only three months? That's incredible!" I was astonished at how far they had come in so little time.

The doors to the infirmary flung open suddenly causing me to jump and Amy to make a surprised squeak sound. The doctor and several uniformed men came crashing through. The doctor led them straight through to the operating room. they were carrying another soldier, he was moaning in pain. I couldn't quite see what was wrong with him but he was covered in blood, that dripped to the floor, leaving a messy crimson trail in their wake.

CHAPTER SEVEN

"Amy, call in the others, we need all hands-on deck here," the doctor instructed before disappearing behind the operating room doors.

"On it, well, guess I got to go." Amy hurried behind the desk and pulled out a hand-held radio. She started to talk quickly into it. That was my cue to leave.

"See you later." I waved before going back to the ward.

Nia came in a short while later with a smile from ear to ear. I made me feel good to see her so happy. She was practically glowing.

"Soooo, you're now looking at the new teaching assistant for our camp." I didn't think it possible but her smile grew wider.

"Wow, that's great, congratulations," she sat in the chair by the side of my bed and handed me the bowl of soup.

"Yep, I'll be working with the younger school age 3 to 5. The guy I'm working with seems so nice, his name is Brian Cook, he was a vice principal at a primary school before all this happened."

She was so excited she went on and on about the job and the staff she had already met during and after her interview.

Said the Captain had another four applicants, two of which were qualified teachers. Because of the positive replies the captain had decided to do a younger class with Brian and Nia running it for ages 3-5, a class for 5-10 and one for 11-14.

It was so nice to hear her enthusiasm that I just let her talk, smiling and nodding when I felt it necessary. I finished my soup and placed the bowl onto the bedside table and poured myself a glass of water.

"It sounds so good, I'm so happy for you. Shaping little minds. I cannot think of anyone better for the job." I smiled feeling extremely proud of her.

"Oh, crap I forgot your coffee, I'll go and get some." Before I could stop her, she was gone; bouncing out through the doors. I chuckled to myself. This job had certainly given her a spring in her step.

I lay back, it was warm in here today. I tried to distract myself from the heat by thinking of Poppy and Cameron. I was trying to think of my family in a positive way but it was hard. I was not to focusing on my loss, but of how lucky I was to have had them in my life even if it was for such a short time.

I must have dozed off for a while. I woke up to her the voices of Nurse Amy and Nia. They were excited whispers.

"Hey, you two," I croaked, my throat was dry from the heat as I slept.

The nurse handed me a single tablet this time which I refused. She didn't argue but instead placed it back into a plastic orange bottle.

She still gave me the water which I accepted gratefully and took a large drink. The cool water felt good as it made its way down my throat.

"Thank you."

"Will and the boys are back George," Nia was almost dancing on the spot from excitement and her eyes sparkled.

"Really?" now I was excited. I couldn't wait to see them. To hear all about their mission. For now, I would have to live through them and their thrilling adventure.

"Yep, I'm just headed there now. Is that ok?"

"Yeah of course it is. Tell them to come and see me and soon," I understood her need to leave me and go to see her uncle. It was one thing to hear that they were back safe but another to see them with your own eyes.

"I will," she skipped to me and hugged me hard. "See you in a bit, I did bring you coffee but it's probably cold now. I'll get you more later, if there's any left."

"See you in a bit." I kissed her cheek

Nurse Amy lingered a little longer. "Is everything ok?" I asked, getting the feeling that she had bad news.

"That soldier we had in yesterday, he turned." She looked nervous and I noticed that her hands were shaking badly.

"Oh no, was anyone else infected?" I was shocked, and scared. This guy was in this part of the camp with us.

"No, he was already in quarantine and was taken care of quickly. But now the men that he came in with and your men have to be put straight into quarantine. From now on the Captain has deemed it protocol that anyone who has been outside of the gates will be placed into a 24-hour quarantine when they return here."

"Makes sense. Do you know if my friends are ok?" I was anxious to find out.

"So far so good, no obvious scratches or bites." She smiled.

"Can I go and see them?"

"I'll have to ask the doctor, I'll let you know soon." She smiled and left the room.

I got up and used the bathroom, washing my face and body the best that I could.

When I returned, the doctor was sat in the chair by my bed, looking tired. Her hair was a mess and she had dark black circles under her eyes.

"How's things doc?" I asked

"Not good George. Did Amy tell you about Corporal lance?"

"Yes, I'm sorry," I didn't know the man personally but any human death was a huge loss to all of us.

She shook her head "I should have seen it, but there was so much damage to his arm and his colleagues swore that he hadn't been bitten or scratched that I patched him up."

"Hey, you couldn't have known, and he didn't hurt anyone, right?" I reasoned.

"No, he was in quarantine at the time. But I wasted medicine on him. Medicine that we could have used for someone who really needs it," there was a little anger in her voice.

"Oh ok." I was a little shocked at her reply.

"I sound bad, don't I?" she asked curling her lip in disgust at herself.

"To be honest, it does sound harsh but I understand what you are saying. I see the need to keep the meds for the more serious of cases. Hopefully Will and the boys have brought you a lot of goods to re stock your shelves."

"Yes, indeed. Let's look at that ankle," I hopped up onto the bed and lifted the leg of my trousers. The doctor started to ease back the white elastic support that my ankle was encased in. It hurt a little but not as much as it had before. Now it was more discomfort than pain.

"Ah its looking good, we should try to get some movement in it. I'm heading over to see the captain. I'm sure you know that his office isn't far from the quarantine area. Would you like to come with me?" she re wrapped my ankle and held her hand out to me.

"Yeah I would love to see them. I'm so jealous that they got to go without me," I took her hand and she hoisted me up with a strength that she didn't look like she had in her.

We started to walk out of the infirmary and towards the

main building. It was late afternoon but there were still many people milling about.

She shook her head disbelievingly. "Most people want to stay well behind the gates, safe behind the men with guns. But you are unique George, you want to be out there fighting the good fight."

I held the door open for her to enter the military main building. We were going to access quarantine out the back from the inside this time instead of my normal route around the exterior.

"Yep, well I'm not most people. I love fighting the good fight. I have this need to get out there and help this camp as much as I can. I need something to take my mind off..." I didn't want to finish my sentence.

The doctor nodded in understanding, we didn't say anything else as we had arrived in front of the rooms where my friends were staying. There was only one problem; Will Billy and Nia were missing.

"Adam. Where are Will, Billy and Nia? You're not sick, are you?" I was worried; my mind went to the worst-case scenario. That Will was injured in some way. That some bloody, decaying undead had gotten hold of him and had sunk their black rotten teeth into his soft warm flesh. That right at this moment Will had been 'Taken care of' and that Nia was now sat beside his twice dead body. Or that Adam was the sick one.

"Hey George, we are all ok." Adam confirmed.

"You're sure?" I had a giant ball of lead in my stomach.

"Yeah don't worry, Billy and Will are in a meeting with the Captain, Nia too."

"Come on George, let's go crash a meeting." the doctor smiled and tugged on my arm.

"Oh, ok that's good thank you. I'm glad that you are all ok. Can't wait to catch up with you both. Tomorrow?"

"Yeah I'll be fine here!" Adam called out jokingly.

The captain's office was at the other end of this large warehouse and through some double doors. As soon as we entered what they were using as the reception area, Rochelle stood up and ushered us into the room without question.

The Captain was sat at his chair, Lt. Jacks was sat to his right. Nia and Will were sat opposite them. There were around eight of nine other uniformed men and women scattered around the room including Billy. They all stood up as the doctor and I entered.

"Ah there she is, we've been waiting on you Annabelle. Welcome George." The captain smiled warmly at us. He pointed to a chair next to Nia for me and the doctor walked around and sat in the chair on his left.

"We wanted to talk to both you and Will, George, Miss Perry here would not leave her uncles side." I sensed that the captain was not too happy about that fact but I knew that nobody would change Nia's mind once it was set. She hadn't seen him in hours and had been worried about him, she wasn't about to let him out of her sight for the moment.

"I'll bet," I looked at Nia and grinned. She just shrugged her shoulders, she had a stubborn look on her face and her eyes flashed, daring me to challenge her.

"Oh then," the captain said a little louder than usual, "We need to get this talk going, I have to leave first thing," he paused letting this information sink in.

"Leave?" I knew that the captain often went on rescue missions with his men when they were short on hands to help but it had been decided by the camp that no more rescue missions could go ahead until the second compound was ready as we just didn't have enough room. The Rescue mission that the men had saved our group was supposed to be their last for a few months.

"Yes, I'm afraid that I must. Let me tell you a little of our back ground," he shook his finger between himself and Lt. Jacks. We were both under the same Colonel, Colonel Rees. Now, for a year before this whole apocalypse started. Even before patient zero attacked that plane full of people over in New Orleans there was chatter in certain military groups. It was said that governments abroad had engineered a mass weapon. Able to kill millions and that nowhere would be safe from this virus." He paused, looking gravely at each of us, in turn, before continuing. "Colonel Rees believed what they were saying and started to order extra supplies for our camp; Ammo and weapons came first. Then six extra generators, extra food and water, clothes and boots even extra bedding. He told his superiors, that the stuff we had was worn and no good anymore."

The Captain paused again, this time to take a sip of water. None of us spoke a word, we were too caught up in his story.

"To be honest, I thought him mad. But I went along with it because we could always use extra supplies at camp. He only ordered bits here and there so as not to raise suspicion. We set the new generators up and placed the old ones into storage. When disaster struck, and blockades started to fall, people were coming to our camp to ask for help. Of course, we took in as many people as we could but we were soon at maximum capacity and had to expand. Within a month the second place was thriving, extra garden patches were made to start growing more produce and people were settling in. We decided that we would try to set up camps across the country. This is the second one that we have tried away from base. The plan is to stay for three months after which a team of five military men would move on with a few trained and skilled survivors to a new place. We bring the basics with us, but mostly we try to get stuff when we are out and about on rescue missions. We also planned to leave at least three military trained men at each base to help to continue training and keep things running smoothly."

"But Billy had other ideas?" my eyes flickered to Billy stood on the left of the captain.

The Captain smiled warmly, "Yes. Billy has proposed that we leave this camp up to the survivors to run. Fully trained personnel are getting rarer and rarer, they would be of more benefit to me out on the road setting up new camps than just sat around here."

It made perfect sense; leave the professionals go head first into danger as they were trained to do and let the amateurs stay safely behind the high fences and brick walls of the compound.

I nodded and gave Billy a double thumbs up.

"Anyway, we were supposed to be having a shipment of goods from the main base, ready for the next camp we are to set up. It's about a seven-hour drive from here in Inverness. That shipment was supposed to arrive three days ago," the captain finished.

"What was the cargo?" Will asked. The captain's eyes flickered to the Lt. just for a second but I caught it. There was something that he wasn't telling us.

"Just a few chickens, some medication, some vegetables that they had managed to grow. They are doing extremely well there, it's what we hope to achieve with this place."

"Ok so maybe they got lost or maybe there's been some hold ups on the road?" Nia replied. She was right, anything could happen out on the roads these days. What may be a few hours' drive could now turn into days.

"Yes indeed, but the strange thing is that we have lost all communication with the other site. Again, this could nothing but I would like to go and check. These are my friends,"

"Ok I get that, if it were these guys I'd be right there with you already planning the mission. But here's my question and please don't feel that I'm trying to be rude here, but why are you telling us?" I looked at everyone else in the room, they were all military and I understood why they would be informed but not why we would be.

"Well, we have been talking with other survivors and as you know we take a statement of everyone's account of what they have been through since the apocalypse began. Just to see what skills people have and maybe even to match up a missing person with their families. When it comes to both, you and Will are regarded significantly high by the people that you were rescued with. Especially Billy, here." He pointed over his shoulder at Billy who smiled at me. "Plus, when asked what jobs you would like Will said sentry duty and the occasional mission and you said supply runs. So, we would like both you and Will here to join our ranks. We are drastically thin on military members at the moment."

I looked at Will, he had a look of utter shock on his face that I'm sure would be mirrored on my own. I'd thought about asking them for a military position but didn't think that they would ever consider me which is why I chose supply runs. It was the closest job which required military training that I thought I could get. Now that I knew it was not the case I was a little excited.

I nodded slightly to Will who replied with his own little nod.

"Sounds good to me," I grinned at the captain, standing up and shaking his hand.

"Me too," Will stayed sitting down but had a huge smile on his face and I knew that he was just as excited as me to become part of the team.

I sat back down and glanced at Nia, she looked tremendously unhappy. I knew why. This meant extra danger for myself and now Will too.

"Right, that's fantastic. I'll be leaving with a group of four officers around ten, I'd like to see you both here in my office at 9am sharp to be briefed. Thank you both." he smiled at us and started to talk quietly to the doctor.

I guess that was our cue to leave. I got up, followed by Nia and then Will. We left the room and closed the door behind us. The rest of the officers stayed.

"Nia, I-" I started to explain why I had chosen to say yes to the captain but she cut me off.

"I understand George, after hearing about what the guys managed to get from the lab I get it. I know how much it will help our camp, I just wish that it wasn't you guys risking your lives, but I guess in this world we are risking our lives every day."

I pulled her in for a big hug, then Will joined in.

"Team hug!" Adam called out running towards us and hugging tightly, I laughed. This felt good, although I felt bad for feeling happy, I couldn't push it away.

"Hey, aren't you supposed to being quarantine?" Nia laughed

"They let us out early, like Will, for good behavior," Adam explained.

Amelia was with him but did not join in our family hug. Instead she held back, hugging herself and looking a little awkward.

"I'm here too," Billy had just exited the Captains office, looking very smart in his new khaki uniform. It suited him.

"That's great, how about we all get some food and you guys can fill me in on what happened whilst you were out?" I said once I had broken free of the hug.

Nia held on to my arm, I watched as Billy's eyes narrowed in jealousy. I wasn't about to tell her to let me go though. She was my friend, if he had a problem then he needed to man up and say.

So, I just ignored it as we made our way towards the

canteen, laughing and joking like we didn't have a care in the world. I tried to hide my hurt that I still carried around behind my smile. My friends had gone out on a mission and had all come back safely and for that I truly was grateful.

CHAPTER EIGHT

Will and Adam were so animated when they were telling the story of their adventure that I couldn't help but feel a little green with envy. I swore that at any moment I was going to turn into the hulk.

Billy didn't say much, just nodded along as he played with his food. He kept giving Nia pointed looks which she kept ignoring, in the end he huffed out an excuse and left the room. Nia looked troubled but when she saw me looking she smiled and started up a conversation with Amelia.

The boys told me that they had started off well and got to the facility quickly. No hordes of zombies, no road blocks with assholes like Deacon around, ready to take advantage of innocent people. They found most of the things that we needed but that there were a few offices they couldn't access without a key card. They had spent a few hours at the site trying to override the system only to be unsuccessful. Still they were clearly happy with their haul, as was the doctor and the captain. They were hoping to go back in the future to see if they could get in using the doctors key card that she had forgotten to give them.

It all sounded amazing, it struck me as a little odd that the Doctor would forget to give them her key card, after she had planned the mission herself. But I didn't say anything, it sounded like the mission was a success anyway and the doc had a lot going on. Which would probably account for the memory slip.

"Aw guys I'm so jealous, I really wish that I could have come with you," I told them as we exited the dinner hall.

"Don't worry G, were not going anywhere without you next time. I'm going to find Amelia she's been working in the gardens today." Adam said.

"Thanks Adam," I clapped him on the shoulder. "I'd better get back to the hospital. I'm not sure if I'm allowed out yet." I smiled, I said good night to them all, hugging Nia and Will before I walked in the opposite direction to them.

My ankle felt stiff and I limped along but it felt much better than it had yesterday. I waved to Nurse Amy as I entered the medical area and she walked ahead of me to the ward and typed in the code to allow me access.

"Thanks Amy."

"No problem George. Get some rest tonight, I hear you're out of here in the morning." she handed me a glass of water and two different tablets from the ones she normally did.

"New ones?" I nodded towards her hand.

"Yes, thanks to your friends, we now have anti-inflammatory tablets, they will help your ankle. I can get you more pain killers if you need them?"

"No, I'm good thanks, keep them for someone who needs them." I popped the tablets into my mouth and washed them down with the water without any more questions.

"So, tomorrow huh?" I grinned I couldn't wait to be free. Not that the hospital wing was much different to lying in bed all day and night in my own room. But at least if I wanted to get up and walk around I could. Plus, the sooner I got out of here, the sooner that I could start training and building on my skills.

I wished Amy a good night and settled down to read. I heard people coming and going but nobody entered the ward. So, I carried on page after page. Before I knew it, I was half way through the book. But my eyes were getting droopy and I was fighting back yawns every few minutes. I put the book down folding the top of the page into a small triangle so I wouldn't lose my place. Then snuggled under the blankets. I'd forgotten to pick up a change of clothes from my room and wasn't about to go outside at that time of night to get them.

So, I huddled under the covers fully dressed. I fell asleep quickly, dreamt of Kelly, Poppy and Cameron. We were having a picnic at our favourite spot high on the mountainside, we flew kites and played ball. Everything was perfect, the food, the sunshine and most of all the laughter of my family. Not a zombie in sight.

I woke up in the morning sad but with a hint of happiness. It was a good dream, but that's all it was, all it would ever be was a dream.

I got up to use the bathroom, without my crutches. I stripped off and washed the best that I could, then dried in the provided towel and got dressed again. I noticed that a disposable razor had been left out for me; biggest hint ever Doc. I thought.

In any case I used the razor, I was starting to look hideously scruffy. I looked much younger and tidier by the time I had finished but I had cut myself a few times and had to use toilet tissue to avoid staining the towel.

One look in the mirror at the tissue dotted on several areas of my cheeks and chin and it threw me back to when my father taught me how to shave for the very first time.

My heart still ached for my parents even after all this time,

I'd lost my mother to cancer when I was just 19. My father followed her six months later from a heart attack. I believe that it was a broken heart after losing my mother. I was brought up by my father's older sister who was like a second mum to me. I lost her two years ago to cancer also. I was glad in a way that they were not around now to witness what our world had become but I also missed the hell out of them and wished for just one more hug off my aunt Sarah or one great big hug off my Mum and Dad.

I shook myself out of my sombre mood. Today was the start of my new job, a chance to do my family proud by helping others.

I tried to style my hair but it had gotten too long so I just brushed it the best that I could and made a mental note to ask the doc or the captain if we had any hairdressers in camp.

I practiced smiling in the mirror and immediately felt foolish. I left before I could think up anything else as silly. It was quiet in the medical centre. A man I didn't know was in nurse Amy's place behind the desk and there was no sign of doc.

"Hi there, you must be George. I'm Ben, the Doc left a note saying to give you these. Take two a day, one in the morning and one in the night." He gave me a small, orangey brown plastic bottle with four tablets in it. They looked like the anti-inflammatory tablets that Amy had given me yesterday.

"Thanks Ben, that's great. So, I'm free to go?" I asked hopefully.

"Yes, you're free to go," he chuckled.

"Great, thanks again. Oh, and before I forget, are there any hairdressers in camp?"

"Yeah, three doors down on the left from the canteen. Lady named Michelle and a guy named Rick I believe." he nodded.

"That's great. Thanks. Bye Ben." I hobbled out of the door as quickly as I could.

I still wasn't walking properly and there was a slight discomfort when I put my weight on it but I wasn't in any pain.

I stopped by the food hall on my way to the captain's office to pick up a mug of coffee to go. I thanked the lady behind the counter and sipped at my coffee, taking care as it was scolding hot.

On my way to his office I took the long way around, choosing the exterior route rather than the interior. Even at this early hour there were lots of people milling about. Tending to the gardening and the cattle. There were people on the sister compound, they had started to erect a fence between the two camps. They had a nice safe walkway so that you would not have to leave the protective fence of one camp to enter the other. The next job was reinforcing the walkway.

I carried on towards the captains' office, not wanting to be late on my first day, but I was still the last to arrive.

"Am I late?" I felt a little self-conscious.

"No, I just got here myself." Will replied, eyeing up my mug. I handed it to him and he smiled gratefully. Taking a sip and moaning out loud.

"You two want to get a room?" I joked.

"Oh, I would love to." Will winked at me and wiggled his eyebrows.

In the room, today was just Will and I, Captain Cooper and Lt. Jacks. The latter two had been watching our exchange with an amused expression.

"Right then, let's get to it, so that Will can go and give that coffee some sweet loving," the Captain grinned.

Will and I nodded and Lt. Jacks chuckled, I loved the Captains humour.

"I'm leaving here in just under an hour. I'm taking a team of four men. We plan to go visit the sister site, and see what's up. I'm hoping it's just a problem with their coms system but it could be that they have been over run. If this is the case we will turn around and come back home. Lt Jacks here will be in charge. You will both start your fitness training today. Any questions?"

"Is it just us two joining the ranks?" I honestly thought that there would have been more people lining up to join.

"Yes, unfortunately most don't want anything to do with the fight. They want to bury their heads in the sand and pretend that nothing is happening outside of these gates. As you know Billy has already joined, the men that came in with you, the mechanics Lewis and John have joined us also. Your pal Adam is going to be sentry and construction, and to be honest we could use his strength for the construction side. All men and women will have the opportunity to go through training if they want it. Most don't."

I nodded, I understood in a way, why they were scared to get involved. The sad thing is that they would need this training to save their lives. They just couldn't see it yet.

"Ok then, I look forward to starting."

"Me too," Will took another long drink of my coffee and handed me back my mug. It only had a tiny drop left in the bottom.

"Gee, thanks," I let all of my sarcasm shine through.

"No problem." he got up and clapped me on the back.

"Sir is it ok if we go and get a proper mug of coffee and change into workout clothes?" Will asked the Captain.

"Of course it is. I'll send Lt. Jack to come and meet you in the canteen in a little while ok?"

"Great thanks," we both got up and left, I followed Will out of the office and through the double doors at the end of the corridor. This brought us into the military living quarters where we currently slept also. Although it was a huge place and our rooms were across the other side.

Will talked excitedly on the way to our rooms, I nodded

along. Too excited to say anything. My mind was in overdrive. I never thought that I would be part of the army. But having something to occupy my mind, something that would benefit my friends, meant something to me and I was going to give it my all.

"George? You still with me bud?" Will snapped his fingers in my face.

"Uh? What? Oh, I'm sorry will I was lost in thought then. I'm pretty excited about this," I snapped back to Will and tried to focus on what he was saying.

"Me too, that's what I was saying. Let's go into your room first George."

I unlocked the door, it smelled like sweat and stale alcohol inside, so I opened the window to let the fresh air through.

"What's up?" I asked a serious looking Will.

"Our 'Gang' had a meeting last night in my room. We discussed what jobs each of us were going to take on. Each of us thinks that it's important to take on jobs that will benefit our group if we ever need to leave here. There was no question of if we will stay together. All of us that left Deacons place and came here are now family. Do you agree?"

"Yes of course. Although I am closer to some of you than others, I would never leave any of them behind." I was honest, as far as I knew these people were the only ones I had left alive.

"That's good to know. So, we along with Billy are training up on weapons and getting fitter, Adam is learning all he can in construction, Kandace is starting in the gardens, learning how to grow fruit and veg and to look after the chickens. Amelia is starting in the hospital. Nia is in the school area keeping an eye on our kids but also has access to all the army's maps on this area. All of our gang are learning new skills." He sounded really positive and his enthusiasm had started to rub off on me.

"It all sounds great. I hope that we will never have to leave here and eventually we can build this up to be a place that thrives. Where we can call home. But I also think that these skills are essential. I also think that each of them need to do a basic survival course, how to build fires safely and shelter. A basic training in weapons too." I was happy that the others were on board and honoured that they cared about me enough to consider me as part of their family.

"The captain has already ordered the weapons training for all members of this camp over the age of 14. They will be taken in groups of eight. I've asked that Amelia and Kandace be in the first groups. Nia has weapons training from when she was in the force."

"Uh wait. Nia was in the police force?" I was shocked. We had never spoken of our lives before the disaster.

"Yep, as was I, for ten years. But that's a story for another time. Get changed ill meet you at the dining hall in ten." he smiled and left my room humming a tune that I didn't know.

"See you there." I called to a closed door. I couldn't believe that they were both in the police force and I didn't know.

I guess once things settled it was a discussion we may have, sometimes the past was too painful to talk about.

I stripped off and got dressed quickly in a pair of dirty grey joggers and a black vest, the only half decent shoes I had were the black boots that the captain had given me and so I put them on.

I left my room, locking the door behind me and made my way to the canteen, I had laced up my boots tightly around my hurt ankle just to give it a little extra support.

Will was sat on the table nearest the door. The room was full of people today. "What's going on?" I asked confused, the canteen was never this full.

"Scrambled egg day, there's not much of it to go around but it's good." Will replied, shoving a forkful of egg into his mouth.

I legged it to the back of the cue, I hadn't been at camp

long but I knew that when there was scrambled egg or anything fresh on offer then you got there quickly.

"Sorry, all gone. We only have dry cereal or self-heating meals left." The woman behind the counter called out. Receiving a load of moans and groans in reply.

"This is bloody ridiculous, it's always the same few that get the food. How the fuck can you run out of eggs. There's a whole barn full of chickens." one man behind me called. A few other shouted out "Yeah." in agreement with him.

I saw the situation going south very quickly, a few people got up and left, not wanting to be in the way if a fight broke out.

"I'm sorry, but they only lay so many eggs per day, we have made as much as we could and it goes on a first come first served basis." the woman from behind the counter explained calmly. She was a large woman with frizzy curly red hair.

"Well, you fat Bitch, go and make some more, I'll wait." he snarled, he sat down on the table opposite the serving hatch and put his feet up on the table. His greasy black hair was tied back in a ponytail, his eyes were so dark that they looked black and he had small, thin lips. He was dressed in military uniform and I could see that it had gone to his head.

"There are no more eggs, it will be a few days now before we can get enough-" he cut her off.

"Go and cook me some bloody eggs now my lovely or you won't want to know what happens if you answer me back again." He stood up and puffed out his chest. A few other men stood behind him, dressed in civilian clothes.

She didn't reply but I could see that she was getting nervous, she pulled down the hatch quickly and I heard the click of a lock from the other side.

The man roared, jumping over the table in one fluid movement and screamed at the hatch, he started to pound on it.

I moved closer to him as people were moving away "Hey

man come on she said that there wasn't any left," I placed my hand on his arm trying to calm him down.

"Who the fuck are you?" he screamed at me, swinging around his arm he hit me on the chin.

"Oh, hell no." I heard from Will behind me as he ran at us. Then all hell broke loose.

CHAPTER NINE

The fight turned into an all-out brawl. They threw punches and then chairs, then fists. Nobody was badly hurt but there were a few bruises and black eyes. It landed us straight back in the Captains office along with officer dick head.

"I'm so disappointed, I do not have time for this. I thought that I could count on you to keep order here, not start a riot!" the captain roared at us. His face had gone completely red and I felt like a school boy again in the principal's office.

"They started it, they are pricks. They don't deserve to wear the uniform." Gary shouted.

"The way you spoke to that woman was disgusting. My friend here was trying to calm the situation and you clocked him one. You pal are the one who doesn't deserve to wear that uniform." the venom in Will's voice gave me the chills. But officer dickhead didn't flinch. He just curled his lip up into a snarl.

"I have spoken to various witnesses and the majority say that you started it Gary."

Oh, so the dickheads name was Gary.

"That's fucking pathetic. They are all wimps. You'll never

win this war with pussy's like them running this place." Gary jumped up and out of his seat causing it to fly backwards.

"Sit down Gary" the Captains voice was low but the tone was harsh.

"You're going to let them takeover this place, and those things will be in here eating the rest of the innocent people before you know it. These two pansy's will run this place into the ground. Let me run this place under Lt Jacks, I'll keep a good law and order here."

"I agree that there are certain ways that things need to be run in order to be successful" the Captain nodded.

Gary's face had turned into a smile, if you can call it that. It was more of a grimace, he looked evil. I still swear that his eyes flickered to full on black before returning to normal.

"But, what we don't need is a dictatorship. I want this camp to work together to become great. We don't need arrogant, chauvinistic people like you. Please give your uniform to Lt Jacks who is waiting outside."

"you're going to regret this, all of you cock suckers are!" Gary picked up his fallen chair and threw it across the room. it didn't hit anyone, but it came awfully close to Will's head.

I looked at my friend, his fists were closed tightly and I could see the muscles bulging in his jaw. He was angry and dying to get up and hit Gary again but was trying to be obedient for the captain.

Gary, flung open the door in temper but it swung back too quickly and before he could react, it hit him in the face.

"Ahhh" the door had knocked him flat on his ass.

I tried to stifle the snigger that was threatening to burst from my mouth but I couldn't, the man got what he deserved. Blood was gushing from his nose and his eyes were streaming water.

"Oh no, it looks like you've broken your nose. Couldn't have happened to a nicer guy" Will said sarcastically, standing up and towering over Gary who was holding his nose and howling.

"Help me you assholes"

"Yeah cause calling us names is really going to convince us to help." I replied sarcastically.

"Please" he begged. Staggering to his feet.

Lt Jacks rolled his eyes and gestured to two of his men to come over and join us. They did so promptly and saluted him.

"At ease men, take Mr. Smith here to the infirmary."

"And Gary, I'll warn you now. Any abuse given to the medical staff and you will be asked to leave. We will not tolerate this kind of behaviour. Am I clear?" the Captains tone had turned to ice although it remained at the same level.

"Yes, yes. Just help me. Please" he nodded his head, blood spattering over the floor.

"Ok, take him" the captain nodded.

The two men escorted Gary away from us as Jacks called out for a cleaner. Gary's friends who had been waiting with Jack's outside the office all got up to follow him.

Rochelle peeked out from behind the Lt.

"Are you ok baby?" the captain asked her softly.

Will and I looked at each other surprised. Baby? Must be his daughter, it makes sense that he would want to keep her close. She ran to him and kissed him on the lips.

Definitely not his daughter then. Will's mouth opened in a perfect 'o' as I'm sure mine did. She must have been around half his age. But who the hell was I to judge?

I was lying in a sleeping bag with a half-naked woman when my wife and children were... no I mustn't think like that. My friends and the Captain needed me to be thinking clearly to be able to help them.

"Uh we will be going then sir" Lt. Jacks said, obviously feeling as awkward as we were.

"What? Oh, uh yes. I'm sorry" the Captain pushed Rochelle

away gently and kissed her on the head. She walked back passed us red in the face. Her lips were swollen and her hair was a little out of place.

I smiled. It was nice that they had each other in this world of darkness. She was his star to guide him home.

"I'm sorry about that" the Captain cleared his throat.

"Come in Daniel please"

Lt Jacks came in and closed the door behind him. The four of us remained standing.

"Do you think that I should stay in case this situation with Smith gets worse?" the Captain looked tired. I think that the worry over his friends back at home base was putting extra years on him.

"No sir. I'll have it under control. I'll ask O'shea and Parker to keep an eye on him in the hospital tonight and then for the next week I'll sign him up for so many training ops that by the end of each night he won't have the energy to shit never mind cause any trouble" he grinned, I had a feeling that he was going to enjoy watching Gary struggle.

"Ok Daniel, I trust you. I know that you can handle this. I shall leave as planned then. You two..." he turned his attention to Will and I.

"Please be good when I'm gone, don't get into any more trouble ok? Our force is thin enough as it is, I don't want to be losing any more members. That being said. Thank you for protecting our kitchen staff, we may need to think about putting protective duty onto kitchen, cattle and barn areas"

We both nodded, I was ashamed that we had caused the Captain grief but not that we had stood up for the women.

"Ok. I wouldn't mind that duty" Will spoke up.

"Me either, maybe we can alternate shifts daily? I'd like to learn how to look after the cattle and we can watch over the kitchen staff whilst we're there"

"Sounds perfect" the Captain smiled.

"Yeah, sounds good to me too, I'm thinking that maybe you wouldn't have to alternate days but rather we could have the two of you guarding. Maybe you can alternate walking the ground every hour? To help out the sentry guards." Lt Jacks said.

"I like that idea" the Captain agreed, nodding his head.

I liked that plan too. I'd get to spend more time with Will, whilst also learning everything that we needed to help the camp to thrive.

"We can hash out the details later." Lt Jacks said opening the door.

I took that as our cue to leave.

"I'll walk out with you gentlemen." The captain followed us out.

"I'll miss you" Rochelle came running out from behind her desk and hugged the captain tight.

"Me too, but I'll be back before you know it." He kissed her quickly and gave us a curt nod.

"Now gentlemen, don't think that you have gotten away with that brawl earlier either. I know it's not your fault but you still need to be reprimanded." He had a slight smirk on his face.

I decided then and there that I liked him.

"10 laps around the compound, stay inside the fences but I want you as far and wide as you can go, George be careful on that ankle. Ok?" he winked

And I didn't like him again "Yes sir" I mumbled walking passed him, putting extra emphasis on my limp. I know that I said I wanted to get fit but ten laps? This compound was huge.

"Yes sir" Will was a lot more enthusiastic about the challenge than I. His green eyes that matched Nia's shade perfectly shone brightly in excitement.

He gave Rochelle another hug and they both spoke their good byes in whispers.

Not wanting to intrude on their personal moment Lt. Jacks, Will and I left to go start our training.

Wills enthusiasm was rubbing off on me, by the time we had gotten to our starting point, I was telling myself that I could do ten laps of this place easily, with my eyes closed and hobbling on my busted ankle.

"Ready. Set. Go" Lt Jacks called, in his hands he held a stop watch.

And we were off. I started off well, my ankle was giving me a little bit of pain but nothing I couldn't manage. The more I ran on it the better it felt, Will left me behind on lap two, I was holding him back. I kept up with my steady pace, trying to think of song lyrics, or trying to guess what was for lunch later. Anything to keep my mind off what my body was doing.

By lap five Will was on his seventh lap, that was my guess anyway. He'd overtaken me twice.

By my lap seven I was on my knees being sick, I was that unfit. It was a slight improvement for me. Around six months ago I probably wouldn't have done two laps.

Before we were advised of the virus and told to stay indoors. I was a retail manager for a small electrical firm for ten years. I was used to lifting heavy objects but there wasn't a lot of cardio involved. My upper body strength was good but anything else was just mediocre at best.

"Ok that's enough running for today. Will, well done. George, try again tomorrow. Get yourself cleaned up and start your duty in the kitchens ok?" Lt Jacks called.

Wil helped me up chuckling. "You ok there mate?"

"Yeah fine" I croaked.

We walked towards the building where our rooms and the canteen were. The army called it building 1, we called it the main building. Not very original I know but we didn't really have the time or energy for making up names.

"Ok, I'm going for a quick wash and will head straight to the kitchen, meet you there in a little while." Will carried on ahead of me, turning left towards his room to get a change of clothes.

"Great" I wiped my mouth on my sleeve and staggered towards my corridor in the living area.

I had a nice cold shower, hearing another person enter the wet room. I wasn't sure if it was Will or not and I sure as hell was not going to be the guy checking out another naked person in the shower. I returned to my room with just my grey towel around my waist and my boots on my feet, to get dressed. There was a knock at the door just as I pulled up my red, cotton underwear.

"Come in" I called, I thought that it was probably Billy or Adam come to laugh at the old man who couldn't run.

"Hey George, I, oh I'm sorry I didn't realise that you were undressed I'll come back later" it was Dr. Annabelle, she started to leave and pull the door behind her.

"Wait, doc its ok. I'm just getting dressed after my uh training this morning." I quickly pulled on a t shirt and dark grey combat shorts.

"Ok, I heard about your run in with Gary. Quite a mess you made of him" she looked at me dead in the eye but I couldn't read her face. I wasn't sure if she was happy or angry that I'd been fighting.

"Uh most of that mess on his face is from when he flung a door open and it came back and hit him in the face." I shrugged.

Her eyes widened in shock and she started to laugh. "Oh, that's not how he tells it. According to him there were people holding him back as you and Will took turns hitting him and it was a door all along?"

"Yep, he was causing trouble in the canteen and treating the staff disrespectfully. Will and I try to calm the situation down only to make it even more volatile. The captain had the three of us sent to his office for a telling off. He has discharged Gary from duty but left Will and I on a trial basis for now."

"Oh, wait until I tell the staff over at the infirmary they will love it. None of them like him and he's only been in a few hours. He's mean and rude and handsy with my female staff."

"Lt. Jacks said that he would be assigning men to watch him whilst he's with you so that he doesn't cause any trouble there." I didn't like Gary at all.

"Yeah he has. I was just wondering what had really happened. I knew Will would never have beaten a man unfairly. Although you two do have those kinds of faces that people want to hit" she giggled and her eyes sparkled.

"No, he wouldn't. he's a good man. You should ask him out" I smiled, ignoring her mischievous jibe.

The doctor turned a lovely shade of pink "I uh don't know what you-"she was going to deny it but when I raised my eyebrows at her she stopped talking.

"Is he seeing anyone?" she asked shyly, looking at the floor.

"Nope, he's free and single" I replied in a sing song voice.

"Ok well then, thank you for your information." She hurried out of the room before either of us could say anymore.

I threw on a pair of old Black Nike trainers which were more grey now but well-worn and very comfy and went to meet Will at the kitchen. My legs were sore and shaky still but I was excited to get there to start the first day in my new job.

When I got there Will wasn't anywhere in sight. I walked up to the woman that we had defended earlier that day.

"Hi, I'm George, I'm supposed to be- oomph" the air was knocked from me as the woman grabbed me up into a huge hug.

"Thank you soooo much for earlier. That guy is such an asshole." She let me go and the air rushed into my lungs.

"No problem. Is Will out the back?" I looked passed her to see a few other people cleaning down the worktops but no Will.

"Uh hell no. I gave him a hug too and smelt him then sent him to shower before he comes back into my kitchen." She faked annoyance but I could see the twinkle in her eye.

"I'm Sheila honey. I run this kitchen with the help of some brilliant people. We look after the animals and prepare the food. I'm told that you will be here to look after us and to learn about our jobs?" she eyed me up and down as if she could tell if I'd be any good just by looking at me.

She was a large woman with frizzy curly ginger hair. Her eyes were the deepest shade of blue that I'd ever seen and I could see kindness in them.

"yep that's what I'm told too. I'm more than happy to keep things running smoothly and to make sure that you and your staff are safe from people like Gary but I'm eager to learn also. I'd love to find out how to take care of the animals that are here and the delicious meals that you make us." I smiled, I was genuine.

Aside from the twenty or so army men and women at camp there was the Doctor and the nurse and then around 23 civilians including my group. But for the small amount of room that we had for living quarters, we were full. All in all, the kitchen did an amazing job of feeding us all on what little food we had.

"We are quite lucky and the General knew a guy who knew a guy that had chickens. We took quite a few from the first camp and brought them here. We have several different types as they lay at different times of the year. This way we hoped that we would at least have a few eggs each day throughout the year. We also plan to breed them as the older they get the less they produce."

"You plan to eat them?" I grinned, my mouth was already watering just thinking of a roast chicken.

"Maybe, when they get old enough and stop laying eggs, but not before." She laughed.

"No that makes sense. I love those eggs." Just the thought of the eggs I'd eaten here had my mouth watering.

Will joined us shortly after and Sheila led us around the animals showing us what they got fed, when and how. It seemed the real strain was getting enough water to keep them hydrated in the hot weather.

I enjoyed the tour and couldn't wait to get hands on with them. Even mucking them out.

"You boys would really help me out if you could clean them out for me?" she looked disbelieving.

I would have done anything to help the camp. Even shovelling shit.

I agreed that I could do it alone, so Will could go and help in the kitchen. Getting ready for the lunch hour as the volunteers were already behind.

I continued to care for the animals for most of the day, only taking short breaks to drink some water. I cleaned up their pens and made them more secure with some wood I found at the back of the barn.

Sheila called me in and gave me my rations for the day. She also supplied me with a can of energy drink. They had three crates stored away for the people who volunteered to help. I swore that I would not utter a word about the secret stash and downed it quickly. It was good.

A few of us met in Will's room for an update on the new jobs that we had all taken on. Everyone was thrilled with their new roles. Nia was so ecstatic with teaching the children that she talked a mile a minute and found it hard to sit still; wiggling about on her seat on Will's bed. We each took turns describing how our day had gone. The tasks we had been given, what we liked and didn't like. Amelia and Billy were not able to make it to the get together. Billy was away with the captain and Amelia was helping Annabelle deliver a baby. I finally fell into bed around 9pm, totally exhausted but content.

You would have thought I hated the job but in fact I loved it. Being with the animals out in the fresh air. Hours turned into days.

I closed my eyes and for a while it seemed as though the world was as it should be, the sun was shining, I could hear people talking quietly as they worked. The children's laughter as they completed their daily exercises as part of their lessons plan.

"George?" Lt. Jacks was stood at the gates of the chicken coop that I was cleaning out.

"Yep?" I shielded the sun from my eyes.

"I need you in the captain's office asap" he turned and walked away briskly without waiting for me to reply.

I placed the shovel that I was leaning on just inside of the barn on my way passed and quickly followed Jacks indoors.

This time myself, Jacks and Adam were in the room along with two other men, Will was missing from the room. Rochelle was missing from reception.

"Thank you all for joining me. George, Adam, this is Hardacre and Rich. Both are volunteers like you who have joined our ranks." I was going to voice a greeting but Jacks kept talking so I just gave a short wave which was returned by both.

"Now, long story short, something has gone wrong with the mission that the captain left on two days ago. We received part of a distress call but before we could get a location it cut out." Jacks looked distraught but remained calm.

I plan to take two teams of men out with me this time in case the first team need help. My men are currently loading up the trucks with weapons and extra fuel. We will be taking Benjamin from the hospital area with us also in case our friends need medical assistance. I would like you to come with us. A few of our other guys will be staying behind to keep watch on this place. Can I count on all of you?" he placed two hands on the desk and looked each of us in the eyes for a few moments.

"Yep I'm all in. Are they ok? Is Billy? when do we leave?" I asked trying to hide my excitement that I would finally get out from behind these fences. But anxious to find out if my friend was ok.

"What George said" Adam replied.

The other two men nodded but not as eagerly as Adam and me. I wondered if they had been out on the road for long or if they were taken straight in to camp number one or two and then moved here.

"Ok, as far as we know they were all ok. We couldn't really tell from the short call that we got. Go get your back packs and then to the kitchen for supplies. Meet back here in fifteen minutes."

Adam and I needed no more telling, we were up and out of our seats in a flash. Heading to our rooms as instructed. On a high, ready for our new mission.

CHAPTER TEN

We left before the fifteen minutes were up, I had run to my room grabbed my backpack and threw in a change of clothes. Nia and Will were waiting on us to give us hugs. Amelia ran out of the doors before we were about to leave and flung herself at Adam.

"You be careful ok? If you get bitten or die out there I'll kill you" she cried.

"I will, I promise" he kissed her quickly.

"Wish you were coming." I hugged Will, then Nia. Squeezing her extra tight.

"Me too but I thought it better to stay here to keep an eye on Gary."

"Yeah, I suppose I'd feel better knowing that you are here" my eyes flickered to Nia quickly but Will caught it. He gave a slight nod of his head that he would keep an extra eye on her.

Once all of our good bye's and well wishes were done, we were off.

It was amazing being on the road again. Wide open fields, not another car on the road; well not one that was moving anyway. There were plenty of cars around that had been abandoned. Some extremely bloody and messed up but I tried not to look too hard.

We were around three hours from camp and we'd not encountered any problems.

Our Jeep was first. John was driving, Lt. Jacks was sitting shotgun. Adam, and myself were in the back. Another, larger truck followed us with an extra four men in, including Ben the trainee doctor. We didn't know exactly what had happened to the other camp and then to our men and had brought him along in case they needed medical care. Our communications had lost them quickly after their sos.

My stomach was rolling with both excitement and nerves, I had the whole bloody zoo inside my stomach rather than just a few butterflies. I needed this sense of freedom, to get from behind that horrid fence. But I was also anxious about arriving at the other compound, I wondered if our men were ok. If they had even gotten to their destination and then a darker thought crossed my mind. What if they hadn't made it?

I shook my head trying to clear away that terrible thought, and concentrated on what the other men were talking about.

"So, what do we know?" John was asking Lt. Jacks. John had come along as Lewis, his partner, had been in the first group to leave with the Captain. So, John had demanded that he come on our rescue mission. Plus, it was always handy to have a mechanic on board.

"At around 13 hundred hours, we received a distress call from the Captain. We're not sure how he is or even where he is. That's all we could get was, camp overrun, we need help. Then just static. It's strange as this was the most secure of camps that we had. I'm eager to get there to see for myself what's happened." Jacks replied, his tone sounding curt and uncaring. But I knew different. I knew that he was worried about the Captain by the way he was making a fist; his knuckles were white.

We all nodded, we'd heard it all before in the meeting that was held that morning. I think that John just wanted to hear it again. Maybe he thought that by hearing the details again he may have picked something up that the rest of us hadn't.

"So, the plan as you know, is to take the same route as they had planned, keeping our eyes open for them on the way, just in case they have turned back or are stranded." Lt Jacks pulled out a pair of binoculars from the small back pack by his feet and looked across the fields to our left, then out to the front.

"Anything?" I asked looking the way he was faced.

"Nothing, a few undead, but not a living soul so far. Wanna look?"

He passed the binoculars back to me, I took them gratefully.

Looking through the binoculars I hated what I saw. Thick black plumes of smoke rose into the sky to my left. The dead roamed through the fields, some walking some pulling themselves along, their legs too damaged to walk.

"Can we stop so I can use the toilet?" Adam asked sheepishly.

"Yeah, this seems like a good a place as any. I could do with starching my legs too. Its bloody hot today." Lt Jacks answered, wiping his brow in his shirt sleeve.

He radioed the car behind to let them know that we would be pulling over. John pulled onto the left-hand side of the road. The men behind us got out of their vehicle at the same time that we did.

We checked the immediate perimeter quickly and gave Adam the go ahead to use the nearest bush. I also felt that it would be a good time to relieve myself because we didn't know when we would be stopping next.

I crossed the road and found a large tree that I could go behind. I had just finished and was zipping up my trousers when I heard it.

A low moan followed by a dragging, scraping sound was coming from my right.

I pulled the large knife from my belt and moved forward slowly. The noise was coming from behind a small bush, I moved around it carefully, wondering why it hadn't attacked me yet. My heart was pounding, and my mouth felt dry.

The rope around its neck was caught in the thorns of the bush, when it heard me there it started to struggle more, causing it to tangle up even further.

This one had taken a substantial amount of damage. It was missing both its eyes and the skin had been shredded on the right side of its face. It had been crushed from the waist down and was missing one leg, maybe it had been run over. We'd never know. The rope around its neck indicated hanging but whether they did it to themselves or somebody did it to them I couldn't tell you. But it was a ghastly sight.

I knelt by the side of it, the smell of decay and rot was overwhelming, I drove the knife through its head, right through the temple. A green/black sludge oozed from the wound as I pulled the blade back out.

I turned and vomited by the side of the second-time dead corpse. Some splattered on the tattered remains of the top the zombie was wearing. I didn't think that it would mind though.

"George, man are you ok?" Adam came around the corner with his hands over his eyes.

"Yeah, just found this" I pointed to the zombie on the floor. He peeked out from behind his hands in case I wasn't decent.

"Uh that's just wrong" he gagged but managed to keep his stomach contents where they were.

"Yeah, let's get back" I got to my feet and staggered a little, the adrenaline leaving my system and causing me to feel a little shaky. We got back to the vehicles which everyone stood outside of looking at a map of the area. They were discussing the route again and possible issues that might arise.

I grabbed my water bottle out of my back pack and took a small swig. Swishing it around my mouth I spat it out and then took another long pull. The water was warm but good.

"Everything ok chaps?" John called, seeing me looking a little green.

Lt Jacks folded up the map and tucked it into his pocket, eyeing me up.

"Yep all good." I replied hopping back into the stifling heat of the car.

John and Jacks got in just before Adam hopped in. "Road Trip!"

I shook my head and smiled at him. He was always so jovial. He was able to brighten the mood in the car just a little.

We travelled on for a couple more hours, each man chatting about their lives from before the apocalypse. I kept quiet, everyone in the car knew of what happened to my whole life before the apocalypse. It was now buried six feet under, back at our compound.

"So, Lt Jacks. What is the name for our compound?" the thought had just come to me. I just called it our compound. The military so far had called it camp three or compound three.

"We just called it compound three. Why?" he looked back at me with a puzzled look on his face.

"Just came to me" I shrugged "I think that it should have a proper name, something motivational. Like Camp Revolution."

"Yeah that's good, we should think of a few names and take them back to camp. Then we can ask people to vote" Adam seemed excited by this idea.

"Yeah, maybe if people name it they will feel more involved and want to look after it a little more."

We threw a load of names around, some were good and some were completely hilarious. It was a welcome distraction from our mission, from the tediousness of the journey.

We settled on four names to take back to camp and agreed

that we would ask our friends when we found them safe. Camp Revolution, Purity, Unity and Crimson.

The closer we got to where Jacks said the second camp was, the more zombies we saw. All heading in the same direction as us.

I stroked the handle of my knife, now back at my waist. Feeling reassurance from its presence. I picked up the binoculars again to check them out. Most were dressed in what looked like night clothes. Some just wore tatters, and no shoes on their feet. Not that it bothered them in the slightest. They didn't feel anything but hunger.

"Turn right here" Jacks pointed to where he wanted John to pull off the road onto a dirt track.

We followed the bumpy road uphill for at least a quarter of a mile, before Jacks instructed John to pull into a small clearing.

"This is perfect, from the road we won't be seen but from here we should be able to see everything that we need to." Jacks got out of the truck and walked to the edge of the mountain.

The rest of us followed, the military men behind us kept guard over the area. Jacks held out his hand for the binoculars which I handed to him.

"Oh shit" Jacks muttered, his face had suddenly gone pale. He handed me the binoculars and walked back to the car, he got in and just sat there, not saying another word.

I held them in front of my face and immediately wished that I hadn't. Zombies had overrun the camp. Men women and children were running blindly, not looking where they were going but rather at what was following them. I watched as a woman and a child got trapped against a wall, three zombies closed in on them. A soldier came from nowhere, and took them out, pushing the mother and child into a door that had just opened before disappearing inside himself. I gave a sigh of relief that they got away but my heart broke for those who were not so lucky. There were bodies strewn everywhere, some were even starting to get back up, ready to join the ranks of the undead. I closed my eyes and held out the binoculars for Adam to take. Now that I listened I could hear the screams and cries for help all mixed together with the excited moaning of the zombies as they chased their fast food.

I too walked back to the car, and got in.

"What can we do?" I desperately wanted to help those people.

"I don't know..." Jacks Stammered. His calm had left him.

"Well think dammit!" I screamed at him, hitting the back of his head rest.

"They were my friends, I convinced them to leave the first camp and come to this one." The emotion in his voice was heart-breaking.

I suddenly understood, he was losing people that he loved. All rationalization had gone the moment he saw the dead tearing through his friends, he was struggling to focus.

"Ok I think I have something. Where does this road lead?"

"Uh, just down the other side and round behind camp."

I jumped out of the car "Everyone get in, John I want you to drive around to the back of their compound. I'm going to try to draw the zombies this way, enough of them that you can get some of those people to safety. I'll follow you down" I pulled my back pack out of the foot well in the back.

"I'll stay with you" Adam jogged towards me.

"No, go with them, keep an eye on Jacks. I'm not sure he will do what needs to be done." I said quietly. He nodded and hugged me tightly. "Be safe G"

It was my turn to nod, I wouldn't make any promises, this was going to be extremely dangerous for us all. But if we could save even one of those survivors it would all be worth it.

My plan was simple, wait for them to get as far away as possible, then I would fire off a few rounds to get the zombies attention. I hoped that once several had seen me and heard the gun fire that the hoard would follow. Leaving just a few stragglers in camp that we could dispose of easily.

"Are you sure about this?" Jacks asked through his open window.

"Yes, you go on ahead, try to free wheel it down the hill to minimise sound. I'll make as much noise as I can to try to draw them up the hill. You go around back and fit as many people in as you can. Just keep me a seat. I shall follow shortly" I tapped the top of the car twice to let them know that they should leave.

"Thank you, George," Jacks called as they rolled away.

The guys in the second truck nodded as they passed by. I counted to 40 slowly, closing my eyes. I tried to drown out the dying calls of the people below.

I saw the car that held John, Adam and Jacks, moving slowly around back. They flashed their lights once to let me know that they were in position. The second truck had held back a little. Ready to provide back up if needed.

I took a deep breath, before I could chicken out and fired a shot into the air.

I watched as one by one their heads turned towards the sound, I stood in plain view of them hoping that at least one of them could see me or even smell me. Who knew how they worked? I let off another shot.

Then waved my arms around like a mad man, their groans got louder, their movements with quicker and they came at me with purpose. I looked through the binoculars, the first line of zombies seemed to have a lot of damage to them, they were decaying a lot quicker. My first thought was that I was glad that I wasn't down wind and that I couldn't smell them. My second thought was if they were decaying, then maybe within time they would just rot away. Back into the earth, twice dead. It gave me a glimmer of hope that we could outlive this. That we could start to rebuild our world.

I watched them for a few minutes, trying to climb the hill, one step forwards then about three back. They only started to gain as the ones behind climbed over the ones in front that had fallen. Even then it was slow progress, they would fall over limbs, get up and then fall over something else. But they never took their eyes off me. Their lunch for today.

I moved away slowly backwards, making sure that they could still see me. I turned and looked into the trees behind me. I hoped that they would continue walking that way, thinking that I had also.

Then I had an idea, I ran as far as I could whilst still being visible to the road and hung a jacket from my back pack on the tree. I was hoping that it would draw them into the trees and away from the compound.

Then I ran as quickly as I could down the hill, hidden in the tree line adjacent to the path that my friends had taken just minutes earlier. Not looking where I was going I tripped over something, falling hard and winding myself.

I rolled over and gasped for breath, my chest burned. My knees stung from where the gravel had shredded my trousers and cut into them.

I looked around, wildly shaking my head from side to side, convinced that I had fallen over a legless zombie like the one I'd killed earlier that day. And that any moment I would feel its jaws clamp around my leg and tear at my flesh. The game over for me.

But it wasn't a zombie, it was a man. Well the body of a man anyway. He wore a doctor's coat, black trousers and smart black shoes. I shuffled away until I could catch a breath, all the while keeping an eye on the body and on my surroundings. I didn't want any nasty surprises.

By the time my breath came back, the body still had not moved. I walked closer to it and saw why; it had a bullet hole in its head. But I couldn't see any sign of a gun around the body, and no obvious or visible signs that he had been bitten.

Had the good doctor been brought out here and murdered or had he simply taken his own life and the weapon had been picked up by another survivor. All these questions I had and they would never be answered.

I had a quick look around in the bushes and trees around the body to see if there was any sign of a bag. Not finding one I continued down to my friends, vowing that one day I would sit down and try to remember some of these lost souls. I would write about them in the hopes that one day in the future, they may teach children about our struggles during the apocalypse of 2015-????? Who knew how long it was going to last.

As I came to the bottom of the hill, I could see my friends fighting off a few undead that were left with various hand-held weapons. No guns and as little sound as possible so as not to draw the horde back to us.

I turned my jog into a run, panting hard. I really need to get fit, was my last thought before I too joined in the fray.

CHAPTER ELEVEN

The fight was short but hard and incredibly messy. Putrefied blood, guts and brains were spewed across the ground. I had to concentrate hard on the one that I was fighting so as not to lose my stomach contents over the floor. I hadn't realized how queasy I was until I saw the inside of a human being.

It lunged at me and I lashed out quickly with my knife, slashing it across the arm and causing it to stumble a few paces away. I spun towards it, the deep gash in his arm not doing anything to slow it down. It came at me again, I stuck out my foot to trip it up and then thought better of it. It could have fallen and bitten me through my trousers. So instead I dropped my back pack at its feet and watched it fall to the ground. This one was quick, freshly turned I thought. Within seconds it was trying to get back up. I put my foot on the back of its head and pushed the knife through its temple. It was harder this time than the first, not as easy as they showed in the movies. However, my blade was still sharp and I managed to get the job done, trying my hardest not to hear the tearing, squelching sound as I gave the walker its peace.

I got up quickly ready for the next one, this time it was a

child, ambling towards me. Dressed in a light blue shirt and now bloodstained jeans. Its throat had been ripped open and I could see inside, blood and bone, muscles and sinew hung from the wound. He had a bracelet on, the type you buy your kids and get their names engraved on them, it was made of a navy braid and the nameplate was silver.

He could have been an older Cameron, I couldn't bring myself to hurt him. Closer and closer he came at me, making a kind of gurgling noise from his throat from which blood still ran.

"I can't, I can't" I cried, tears running down my face. Not sure if I was warning my friends, or telling the dead boy or hell, even telling myself.

He lifted his arms as he got closer, ready to grab onto me and make sure I didn't run away. I couldn't run, my feet were rooted to the floor. This was someone's baby boy, they had held him close and somebody had kept him safe and well dressed for this long.

What the hell had gone wrong at camp 2?

"George" Adam, came out of nowhere and swung his baseball bat, hitting the child clean off its feet.

"No!" I called out before I could stop myself. Reaching out my arm as if to help the child.

Adam brought his bat down twice upon the child's head, caving in its skull. Every sickening bone crush made me wince and feel physically sick.

"George?" Adam looked at me, concern marring his handsome features.

"I'm sorry Ad, I... and Cameron, and-" I couldn't form the sentence. But I didn't need to. He got up and pulled me into a tight bear hug.

"It's ok G, I get it. I got your back man. Come on let's get inside."

"Ok." We started to follow the rest of our group towards the main building where we hoped there were survivors.

"Oh, and Ad, Thanks man" I clapped him on the shoulder and lined behind the rest of the men.

"Right, I'm not sure what we will find in here men. The layout is similar to our own at camp three. I'd like us all to stick together and have each other's backs. We have left our two drivers in the vehicles just at the back of the building ready for a quick getaway, should we need it" Jacks told us in a hushed voice.

"Right, let's go and see what we find" Adam replied.

He reached out and knocked the door, tap tap tap then paused then tap tap again. I assumed it was to prove to any survivors inside that we were not the walking dead.

"Hello?" came a small frightened voice.

It was female but I couldn't tell whether old or young.

"Hi there, this is Lt Jacks. We've come to help you but we gotta move quick"

We could hear a discussion behind the door, before another stronger deeper male voice returned "Danny? Daniel Jacks?"

"Yes, it's me, we're looking for Captain Cooper"

We exchanged relieved looks when we heard the door locks click.

We hurried into a small entrance, which used to be a waiting room of some sorts. People of all ages were sat on the chairs and on blankets on the floor.

An older man, with very dark skin and eyes so dark that at first, I thought they were black came and hugged Jacks tightly. He too wore a military uniform.

"It's so good to see you. These things have been attacking us for three days. We have lost a lot of people and we think all our livestock. Ripped to bits. We couldn't get to them quick enough." His eyes went blank as he stared into space, reliving the horrors that he had seen.

"Are you all clean here? Have you seen the captain?" Lt Jacks asked his voice hurried.

I turned to look around, people were crying and hugging each other. A few had on bloody clothes but I couldn't tell if any of them had been bitten.

"Clean?" the man asked, confused.

"Yeah Frank, I mean has anyone been bitten or scratched?" Jacks explained.

"No, no of course not" he looked at us but his sincerity didn't reach his eyes. He was scared and rightly so.

"Do you have access to vehicles and fuel?" I asked, I wanted to get out of here and look for our friends.

"Uh yes, they are kept around the back." He pointed to some navy double doors behind him.

Of course, they were, I shook my head. "Do you know if it's safe?"

"We don't know, not for sure. Its why we are all still holed up here."

Well there was a little honesty at least.

"George?" Jacks nodded right twice with his head indicating that he wanted to speak to me.

"I'm going to take John and Frank and look to see if they have a vehicle large enough to take them all. Can you and Adam make your way to the canteen storage area and collect what you can from there? We don't have the manpower to make this compound safe at the moment."

"Ok"

"Right, here's the plan..." Jacks continued with our plan as everyone else listened.

"Will we be able to get our belongings?" one woman asked.

I looked to Jacks who nodded his head. He sent most of the adults along with two of the men from the other car. Leaving in the reception area, two women, and old couple already carrying small tan coloured backpacks and around seven children.

"Ben, can you stay here and look after these whilst we go do our thing?" Jacks smiled.

"Yep no problem boss. I mean sir" Ben smiled back and held up his baseball bat, already stained red and brown with blood and other fluids I'd rather not think about. He walked over and locked the doors that the others had just left through and tilted the vertical blinds once again.

I nodded to Ben and indicated that Adam should go before me, he followed Jacks through the door who followed John and Frank.

We entered a long white corridor with several navy doors lining it on both sides.

"Right, is any one injured?" I heard Ben ask from behind me before the doors closed.

"I just don't know how it happened..." I heard Frank telling the story from up in front.

I zoned out and concentrated on my surroundings, after the second door on the right was a smaller corridor and at the end of that was a fire exit. These days it was always good to know where the exits were.

We stopped about halfway down the corridor in front of two double doors, that had glass panelling in the top half.

"This is the canteen boys, the storage room is through the kitchen and on the right, you should find backpacks on the bottom shelf. Be careful."

I nodded, pulling out my knife, I took the one door as Adam took the other. We stood facing each other. I knocked on the door loudly, hoping that if there were any undead then they would show themselves.

We waited a few minutes until we could no longer hear the voices of Frank, Jacks and John.

Then we entered slowly, each of us opening the doors wide. Like a cheesy zombie movie in slow motion.

We stood and listened but couldn't hear anything. So, we continued towards the kitchen and to the back room.

It was lined with shelves of tins and dried pasta and rice. They also had a few crates of bottled water. It was like a gold-mine. "Take everything you can carry and more. Hopefully Jacks and the others will come back this way and help us to take more supplies."

We filled the eight worn backpacks with as many supplies as they would take and placed them by the main doors ready to be taken.

I went back through the kitchen, shoving what I could into my pockets; a few breakfast bars and some toothpaste; Adam copied, once we were full, we went back to the main doors and picked up three backpacks each. One on our backs one on our front and one in our hands. They were so heavy with tins in that I struggled to walk. There was no sign of Jacks or John in the corridor so Adam and I walked back to the reception. The rest of the people had also returned carrying their own back packs.

Adam took one person from each family back to the kitchen to help with the extra backpacks and water. He allowed them two tins each for their backpacks and a bottle of water for each person. We kept a crate which Ben and the other military guys took back along with the back packs of food to their truck which was the largest.

The rest of the water we shared out between ourselves, Jacks and John returned whilst Frank came around the front in a large SUV with huge bars across the front.

We met him out front, now on high alert, checking in every direction, just waiting for the horde to return.

"Lee, Tom can you go and get the other truck? We've checked it out and all is good" Frank called out to two middle-aged men wearing jeans and checked shirts. They just nodded and turned walking away without saying a word.

"Frank, you clear on where camp three is?" Jacks asked helping the old couple into the SUV, another man and two women with two kids got into the back also.

"Uh yeah I think so" Frank did not look like he knew.

I looked at Adam who shrugged "I'll go back with you" he spoke up.

"Thank you. That's good of you. Will you have enough men to go on ahead Danny?" Frank asked.

"Yeah, we have enough, Adam are you sure?" Jacks asked walking towards Adam.

Lee and Tom came around the corner slowly in two trucks and the rest of the survivors got in. To go from a full camp to less than fifty people was heart breaking.

"Yeah all is good. If I go back with them then the people back at camp will let us in. If I don't then they may not let them enter." Adam explained his thoughts behind volunteering to leave us.

"Ok man, be careful ok. I don't need Amelia on my back cause you've gone and gotten yourself bitten" I joked, but he knew that I cared about him and this was my way of saying it.

"Love you too George" he hugged me hard and jogged over to the first car.

"Let's go!" he hopped in and tapped at the door through the open window.

I watched as they drove away, and for some reason I felt better knowing that Adam was headed home. Now I just needed to find Billy and the Captain and take them home.

"You ready George?" Jacks called, already heading to our car.

"Yes sir" I replied joining him.

We carried on our journey mostly in silence, horrified by what had happened to camp two and more eager than ever to find our friends safe.

"John, pull over here, we are about half an hour away from our camp. We have to go off road again. There is no safe place for us to view this camp." Jacks' voice woke me from a light sleep.

I stretched and looked around, all seemed quiet. Opening my water bottle that I had placed on the seat by the side of me I took a long drink.

"Have you noticed anything strange?" Jacks asked, his question didn't seem to be directed at anyone.

"Not really, but I just had a small nap" I told him honestly.

"Yeah, we haven't seen any zombies." John replied.

"Jacks, come in Jacks" the radio crackled, from the men in the truck behind us.

"Jacks here, what's up?"

"We have someone approaching our truck"

"Dead?"

"No, living. The infrared camera is picking it up. Two bodies coming towards us slowly."

"Ok, understood. Be prepared for an ambush, driver stays in the car, the rest of you out. Over" Jacks replied.

"Same here, John stay in, keep the engine running in case we need to get away. George, you're with me."

I pulled my gun out of my bag and checked that it was loaded. Then hopped out of the car. It was surreal how easy and natural this now came to me.

No words were used, just hand movements. Jacks indicated that he wanted me to go one way and that he would go the other. John stayed in the jeep. We stood with two men facing one way, two the other way.

The bushes facing Jacks and I started to rustle, the man from the back stealthily moved around, pointing his gun towards the sound. My heart raced, adrenaline pumped through my body. I tried to steady my shaking hand as I aimed my weapon out in front of me. "Please don't shoot" a disembodied voice came from the bush.

I knew that voice, but couldn't place it straight away.

"Throw out any weapons you have and come out with your hands up" Jacks called out in a menacing voice.

"We are unarmed, there is only myself and this child. Please. We need help "the voice begged.

The voice finally clicked, "Lewis?" I called out, now certain that the man in the shrubbery was my old friend.

"Yes, who's that?" he asked poking his head out a little.

"Oh my God, Lewis its George you're safe man. Put your weapons down" I called out as he came out of the bush pulling a small boy behind him. He was smiling like an idiot whilst also checking out the guns pointed at him.

"Put the guns down" I said through gritted teeth. "This is John's partner"

"John? Is he here?" I could see the hope light up Lewis eyes.

"He's right there" I pointed to our car.

Lewis broke into a run "John? John?" he got to the car as John got out, they flung themselves at each other hugging kissing and crying. The little boy had followed him and when Lewis realised he pulled him into the hug too.

"Alright then, let's set up a perimeter and find out what he knows." Jacks instructed the men. Who nodded and got to work quickly.

"Lewis? Can you tell us what happened? Where are the Captain and the rest of your team?" Jacks asked, interrupting the happy re union.

"We were ambushed just before we got to the camp. Most of our team succumbed to the zombies. The Captain, Billy and I managed to get back to my car where a driver was waiting but he had been bitten badly. He tried to drive us to safety into the other camp but turned during the drive and we crashed through the camps fences. We made it to safety but not before their camp was under attack, we got to the radio station and made the sos call to you."

"And you two are all that's left?"

"No there's about 30 people in a barn about 5 minutes that way" he pointed back the way he had come from.

"Well, we can fit two in our Jeep. Two in with Ben in the car behind and the rest will have to try to fit in the flat bed. It will be a squeeze but we should be ok."

"You two get in with John. John turn the cars around and get ready to leave. Give them food and water from the back. We will go and get your friends Lewis."

"You two, George. Let's go. Ben, you too we may need medical assistance"

We moved quickly through the grass, I could see the huge barn from where we started. I couldn't wait to see Billy and get him home safe. When only Lewis emerged from the bushes I thought that we had lost Billy and the Captain.

There were screams and shouts. We suddenly saw people running from the barn just seconds before a huge explosion hit us off our feet.

There was a ringing in my ears, I had landed hard on my back, it stung from where the solid ground had grazed my skin, and I was slightly winded.

"George? Are you ok?" Jacks was staggering towards me, holding out his hand to help me up. I could hear him but his voice sounded far away and muffled. I nodded, not sure if I could speak just then.

"Let's go and see if there are any people left to help" he yanked me to my feet and held me for a few seconds whilst I got my balance back. We checked and saw Ben and our other men getting back up onto their feet. Without hesitation, we ran towards the fire hoping that we would find the Captain and Billy safe.

CHAPTER TWELVE

By the time we got to the barn, there wasn't much left to find. Jacks disappeared into what was left of the building before I could stop him. Ben and the other men stopped to check on people. I continued around the exterior. About half way around, a low guttural moan stopped me. My hearing was coming back to normal but was not as it should have been. I stood as still as I could, moving only my head from side to side as far as it would go. Until finally I turned to face back the way I had just come, but I couldn't see anything but trees. I had a terrible feeling in my gut, something was telling me to look up. I think it was paranoia rather than experience.

And sure enough, stuck up in a tree was one of the undead, tangled in its branches with not enough brain power to work out how to get down. What was left of its clothing looked a lot like my military gear and selfishly I hoped that I it wasn't someone I knew.

"Hey" Jack's voice startled me and caused me to jump. I turned to look at him just as the main branch holding the zombie snapped causing it to fall. The body landed with a hard thud and I could have sworn that I heard the crack of ribs breaking, maybe and arm too. But it wasted no time in pulling itself towards me, trying to get a taste.

Jacks walked up behind it and held his knife above its head. It didn't even notice because it was so focused on me. He knelt and thrust his knife through the temple, he made it look a lot easier than I had done it earlier that day. There was no shout of alarm, or squeal of pain, just a sort of angry grunt that it had been stopped from its final meal. Just for a second or so as the knife sliced through its skin and into its brain, or what was left of it anyway.

I closed my eyes and remembered back to the beginning, well a few months in, when that's all we had left was radio. They encouraged us to stay indoors, lock all doors and windows and stay out of sight. But if we were attacked then we were to attack the head and try to destroy the brain.

Kelly and I had discussed it one evening, over candlelight when the kids had gone to sleep. We had both agreed that shooting someone in the head or worse, having to stab or beat them to death in the head was something that neither of us could see ourselves doing. How that had changed. Now if it needed doing I could do it, I never took enjoyment out of it but if it was down to them or myself and my friends then the zombies would lose with their heads destroyed each and every time.

I closed my burning eyes, breathing through my mouth, trying hard not to smell, the acrid burning of flesh. I could hear the crackle as the fire made its way through the dry grass and trees.

"George, I'm sorry for your loss" I opened my eyes and met with Jacks' looking sorrowful.

He held out a pair of dog tags and then knelt to the floor to go through the pockets of the now still body.

I turned over the tags in my hand, B.S was crudely scratched in. Billy Sanders.

My heart was in my stomach, we were too late. How in the hell was I going to tell Nia that I wasn't good enough to save her friend? Jacks handed me another set of tags. These had been engraved with the Captain's initials and were a lot more worn than Billy's had been.

"Found them in the breast pocket of Billy's shirt."

"I guess that's our answer" I voiced out loud, my voice breaking. I had honestly thought that we would have found them alive and well and ready to come home.

"Yeah" Jacks had fallen onto his backside in the grass, his eyes were wide and glassy. The captain had been his friend also.

"I'm sorry" I clapped him on the shoulder.

I could see Lewis and John running towards us with weapons in hand. Ben just behind them carrying his doctors bag.

"We better go" I nodded towards our friends. Jacks followed my gaze and nodded getting up slowly.

They stopped when they saw the looks on our faces.

"Billy?" Lewis asked.

I shook my head.

"None of the others survived, sorry" Ben told us.

"Your other men went back to the car when we came running to try to call for backup" Lewis told Jacks.

The five of us carried on walking back towards our cars, each lost in thoughts and grieving for our lost ones.

The little boy had stayed with the other army men and ran to Lewis as soon as he saw him. Hugging him tightly, burying his head in Lewis' chest.

Jacks went to let the other men know our situation whilst John and Lewis got our new little friend Cory, comfortable in the back of the car. Ben didn't say another word he just got into the back of his truck.

Followed by the soldiers, Jacks came walking back to us, head high. "Let's go home gentlemen. I have a base to look after now." His face was wet and his voice somber.

We all nodded, he got in on one side of the child and I got in the other; no car seats anymore. John and Lewis took the front seats, holding each other's hand as we pulled away.

John did a three-point turn and started to follow the other truck. He drove for as long as he could without putting the lights on. When it was too dark to see, we pulled over and took it in turns to keep a lookout. Cory, slept throughout the night, I placed my black fleece jacket over him. The poor boy must have been exhausted, god only knows what he had been through. Lewis said that his family had been in the camp when they were over run and Cory's father had begged Lewis to take Cory to safety whilst he and his wife stayed to fight. That was the last they had seen of them. I wasn't sure what was worse, knowing that your family was dead or not knowing.

I took my watch post just as dawn was breaking. I made sure that everyone was safely in our car and instructed the driver behind that we should leave asap. I was eager to get back home. To make sure that Will, Nia, Adam and the rest of our people were safe.

Jacks who had now taken the front seat woke up groggily. "What the?" he looked around, squinting at the bright sunlight.

"Go back to sleep, I'll drive for a while. I just wanted to get home quickly" I spoke quietly, careful not to wake anyone else up.

Jacks grunted a reply and lay his head back against his seat. Within moments his low snores filled the car.

John and Lewis had moved to the back seat with Cory, each of them embracing the child as they slept.

It was kind of peaceful driving on the open road like that, everyone sleeping, the only other moving vehicle was the one in front of me that I was following back to home camp. There was peace in this new world, there was still beauty if one cared to look past the rotten flesh and dead people walking.

We stopped again after a few hours for a bathroom break. Everyone was awake although still extremely quiet. Each if us thinking about our loved and lost ones. Lewis took over driving, I was in the front with him and Jacks, Cory and John stayed in the back playing eye spy. I knew that it was the last thing that Jacks wanted to be doing but he did it anyway, knowing that Cory had lost a lot of people too and that it was harder for him.

"Heads up, there are trucks coming towards us" the crackle of the radio informed us.

I grabbed up the radio quickly as Jacks and John checked their guns.

"How many?"

"Uh, we see three" came the reply.

"Ok start slowing down. We don't know if they are friend or foe. Get your weapons ready" Jack instructed me.

I repeated Jacks message, word for word as he told me.

The trucks stopped, still facing us, and for a while nobody got out. Then the driver's door on the front truck opened. Will stepped out and held up his hands. I was out of the car before anyone could stop me and was running towards him. I knocked him over with a bear hug. Even though it was only a few days since I had last seen him I had missed him, I had missed them all and the loss of Billy had only strengthened that longing to be amongst my friends again.

We landed on the floor with a thud, quickly joined by Nia and Adam and eventually a very reluctant Amelia. We all just sat there on the dusty road, hugging and crying. We finally checked the perimeter and set up a camp fire to boil some water that we gathered in a nearby river to try to save our bottled water.

We told them of our adventure and wept with them when we told them of the previous teams demise all except for Lewis. We grieved as a family, hugging and comforting each other.

Their group was made up of Nia, Will, Adam and Amelia. Mr. and Mrs. Snow, an elderly couple whose name matched their hair colour. They seemed jolly and nice enough. They had with them their granddaughters who I vaguely remembered seeing back at camp two when we rescued them. They were called Maddie and Amber.

Another couple, the Price's, Heidi and Andrew. They had five children, Molly was 15, Leo was 14, twins Paisley and Peyton were 9 and the youngest was Ollie who was 7. Molly was their child and Leo was their nephew, the other children they had taken in as their own when the little ones had lost their parents.

In the third and final truck was Frank, Jack's friend from camp two, Brian Cook, Nia's teacher friend and the chef and my new friend Sheila.

"What Happened?" I asked after all the introductions were complete.

"Bloody Gary, that's what. As soon as you guys left he rallied his men and they took over. There was just too many of them to fight, I'm sorry Lt." Will explained.

"We started putting some food and water away and talked to our group about leaving. Most wanted to stay. They are blinded by what they think is a safe place. But Gary will run that place into the floor." Nia chipped in. She looked angry and hurt, I could see the fire in her eyes.

"That asshole. I'll show him when I get back" Jacks also looked annoyed. I knew that he wouldn't take any nonsense off Gary. I just hoped that there was a camp left when he arrived.

"We decided to leave. He made it clear that we are not welcome back" Adam told us.

"Ok then, what's our plan?" they knew that I would not leave them behind.

"We don't know yet, we understand if you would like to go back to camp and try living there in relative safety." Nia said, she looked at me and then bowed her head.

"What? And miss all the zombie fun out here on the road? Never!" I grinned at her. She looked up, smiled crazily back at me and ran into my arms.

"Yeah us too" John and Lewis agreed nodding their heads. Lewis pulled Cory in close.

I guess that they were taking the boy in. My heart grew two sizes larger for them, they would make amazing fathers.

"I'm going to go back to camp and see if I can straighten things out. I'll need to check on Annabelle and Rochelle." Jacks told us.

I wasn't going to try to talk him out of it, he had a duty and nothing would get in the way of it. So, I just nodded.

"I'll go back with you Danny" Frank said.

"I uh, know of a place we can try. A friend of mine called me at the start of this damn apocalypse and told me of a secure location. The only reason we haven't tried it before now is because we have never travelled this far North. But since we're already halfway there should we try?" John asked. He hadn't given us a lot of information about the new location to make our decision but since nobody else had any other ideas then we agreed that we would give it a go.

It was decided that we would keep the largest of the military vehicles to take with us. Jacks and his two men along with Frank kept what food and water that they needed for the drive home and gave us the rest to go on with. Nia and Will showed me the loot that they had left with.

"Ok then, let's go. Jacks be careful, please. You know where we are headed should you need to find us" I hugged him. Daniel Jacks was a good man, a man I had come to like. I knew that he needed to go back and see if he could save the camp but if they didn't choose to come with Will and his group then maybe they didn't need saving. Maybe they were happy to sit back and let Gary tell them what to do and how to live.

"See you again. I hope."

We watched them drive away until the dust settled. I was excited to be with my friends again. Even though not all of us that had escaped Duncan's crew was here I had the most important ones. I vowed that one day when this was all over that I would go back and visit my family. My heart ached for leaving them behind, along with my precious album of family photos.

I gave Nia Billy's dog tags, she didn't say anything, just hugged me tightly and got into the back of the car. I hopped in too, a little fired up for the journey ahead.

There was excited chatter from everyone. We didn't want to have left camp three and some of our friends behind. I was going to miss Kandace, Annabelle and nurse Amy the most. Annabelle, the doctor, had chosen to stay behind to help those who needed her there. For that we were sad but for the adventure ahead, the journey into the unknown, of what we would discover next, we were all tremendously happy and excited.

We arrived at the destination that John had led us to after three days, not trusting to drive in the dark. We would pull over then take it in turns to sleep, there were also a lot more road blocks along the route. Set up by the military to try to control the situation, now long abandoned.

We had travelled miles across the country and still had not seen another living person. There were plenty of undead, however these ones seemed even slower than the others.

The place looked amazing, thick, high fences covered in barbed wire. Two exits; one East and one West. Massive gates on wheels, covered in hard wooden boards.

We drove around it three times to check out the security, there were a few shamblers around but otherwise all was quiet.

We stopped our cars at the West gate just next to the security cabin. Nia was driving our jeep; we had been taking it in turns to drive, each of us exhausted but knowing that we had to keep moving as far away as possible from camp three.

Will radioed the cars behind "keep your engines running for now, John can you come and join us up front? Over"

Quiet static returned, Will slipped it back into his shirt pocket. Today he wore what were once dark denim jeans but were now quite faded, a black shirt, and black boots.

John joined us in front of the gate and knocked on it loudly. Will and I kept an eye out for zombies.

Nobody replied, John pulled at the latch on the gate but it didn't open.

"It's padlocked from the other side, I may be able to get a bolt cutter through." He ran to his truck and back to us quickly. He looked excited, I smiled at him.

"always wanted to try it" he explained sheepishly.

There was a satisfying clunk as the chain broke and then the clatter as it swung down along the inside of the gate. He looked smug and grabbed hold of the gate, pulling it open with two hands. It was on wheels but extremely large and heavy and so it took some effort. Normally it would run on electric, now it ran on man power.

John was putting all his energy into opening it as Will checked out our surroundings. Neither of them saw the gun.

"Duck!" I screamed.

Both of them used to training now hit the deck quickly as I ducked behind the fence as a bullet whizzed past us.

"I don't want no trouble, turn around and leave. Or I will shoot" a gruff sounding voice called out, it was followed by a sickly cough and the gate being heaved closed again. We all looked at each other in shock. We should have expected the response we got but we had thought we would have been welcomed with open arms. My heart was pounding from the shock of the gun firing at us.

"I'll take care of this" John boldly walked up to the closed gate and banged hard on it three times. He reminded me of the wolf from the three pigs story; I just hoped that he didn't end up in a stew.

CHAPTER THIRTEEN

"I'm looking for Mick. He told me if I was ever in trouble to come here. My name is John, is Mick here?"

"John? John Simmons?" the voice returned.

"Yep that's me. Can you tell Mick that I'm here?"

"Come on in son" we heard the gate open further. Followed by another coughing fit.

John got up and walked through the gate with a wide grin on his face. "Mick, you old coot, you nearly shot me!"

"Eh, wouldn't have killed ya. Can't be too careful these days." He grinned, still wheezing.

"Can we come in? all of us?" John gesture to the three cars behind me.

"Yeah bring your folks in, there's only me here" Mick was racked by another coughing fit that nearly brought him to his knees.

"Mick" John was worried. He held up his old friend as Will called in the rest of our people. The car and two trucks parked just inside the gate.

Mick was sat in one of four golf carts by the first house that we could see. John handed him his water bottle.

One by one our people got out of their cars or trucks. We stood still and looked around, amazed. There seemed to be a whole town inside these walls. It was a beautiful and serene place. So quiet.

"Where's everyone else?" John asked Mick, looking around.

"Nobody here but me. Shit hit the fan on the weekend when I was on duty" he stopped to take a deep breath.

I could hear the wheeze from where I stood. I looked point-edly at Ben and he hurried towards Mick with his medical bag in hand.

Whilst he saw to Mick, John came to explain to us.

"This is a movie set, Mick there was head of security. Once this place is locked down tight its locked down. So maybe we will be safe here for a while."

"sounds amazing"

I was excited, I couldn't wait to have a look around. I remember there being a huge fuss about this movie to be filmed in the Welsh mountains. A huge Hollywood star was coming over and only the best security would do.

Will pulled the gate closed. I could see him huffing and puffing as he pulled the heavy gate across. Just went to show how strong Mick was.

Ben came over to talk with John to advise him on Micks health.

"Hey this is fantastic" Nia came up behind us and twirled in a circle, looking at the stunning old houses that lined the street.

"Only a few of the houses, the town hall and the Police station are real buildings. Most of the stuff inside are just props. I've been staying in the first house there." Mick paused and looked towards us, taking a few deep breaths. It still sounded ragged though, and caused him to cough uncontrollably.

I looked to Ben who was still talking with John. It wasn't looking good. There was a lot of head shaking and frowning.

"Feel...Free... to. Look...around... anything you need" he was getting worse.

"I'm going to take Mick indoors with Ben. You guys go look around. We can stay as long as we want." John and Lewis placed their arms around Mick and took him into the house he had made his own. The rest of us broke off into small groups to look around our fake town.

I was with Nia and Will, Mr and Mrs Snow followed behind slowly. We walked from one end to the other. It was a huge place that mimicked a real town. It had a real park which now had our handful of children in. The Snow's decided to sit on the bench and watch the children play. Revelling in their laughter. For the first time in months the children were allowed to act like children.

There was also a mini golf course. I hoped that one day soon I could get in a few rounds.

My golden find for the day was far across the set, close to the left-hand wall. Three huge trailers. The ones that the stars can rest in when they are not filming. I was so excited to get a look inside that I grabbed Nia by the hand and practically dragged her along. Will jogged to keep up with us.

I tried the door of the first trailer but it was locked, I made a mental note to ask Mick if he had keys to it later.

The second trailer door swung right open nearly knocking me off the metal steps I used to reach it. I stuck my head in quickly then back out, I couldn't hear anything or smell any decay. The door to the bedrooms and bathroom was closed. I stepped inside, knife ready and moved about slowly but loudly. Still nothing returned, all was quiet.

"Seems safe so far" I called out to Nia and Will who had waited outside.

"always wanted one of these" Nia entered first followed by Will.

"Then m'lady this shall be yours" I smiled and gave a small bow.

Will knocked at the bedroom door and listened. "You ready" he looked at me.

"Yep" I nodded.

He opened the door that led to the bedrooms and bathroom. All of which had their doors wide open. He went first checking out each room as I followed.

"Wow" it was amazing.

There was a double bedroom, a bunk bed room and one family sized bathroom.

"Oh my god. It's hers!!" Nia was in the double bedroom looking inside the sliding glass doored wardrobe. She was referring to the huge Hollywood starlet that was lead in the film. Beautiful and expensive clothes and shoes filled the whole of the wardrobe space.

"Knock Knock, any one home" Adam called out sticking his head through the door.

"Come in man" I called. He had Amelia with him holding her hand.

"Me, you have to come and see this" Nia Squealed still inside the bedroom.

Amelia went into the bedroom following the sound of Nia's silvery voice. And then ensued the excited chatter.

Adam looked at Will and I confused.

"Don't even ask man" I laughed.

We sat at the table in the living area/kitchenette and chatted away as the girls put on a fashion show for us. They looked so happy. For the first time in ages Nia's face had a little colour to it and she was beaming. As was Amelia.

Will and Adam went to check out the other two trailers that neighboured this one. I went through the cupboards in the kitchen and found two of them full of protein shakes and bars. I made the mistake of opening the fridge and nearly vomited at the smell and sight of the rotten food within. Well at least we had the shakes and bars that we could share out.

Adam and Will came back in through the doors each eating a bar like the ones I had found. They placed three on the table, one for me and each of the girls.

"There's cupboards full of this next door and a small fridge in the bedroom filled with bottled water." Adam grinned.

"I have a crazy idea..." Will started. Looking between the four of us.

"What?" I enquired, Will had an excited look on his face also. I don't think I'd ever seen a look like that on his face before.

"What if us five take this trailer? Adam and Amelia can take the double, Nia and I in the bunks and you George out here? We can get the Snows to move in next door as its all on one level and smaller than this one." He was so animated that we all got swept up in the excitement of having a beautiful, safe home. One where we may be able to grow old and hopefully outlive the zombies.

We exchanged hugs and each of us had wide grins on our faces. We decided that Will and Nia would go immediately and find the Snow's to show them the trailer and that Adam, Amelia and I would go and ask Mick if it was ok that we have the trailers to stay in.

Adam and Amelia walked on ahead, Nia and Will in the middle and I trailed behind. Watching my friends, happy, laughing and joking. The familiar painful feeling returned to my chest as I thought of the people we had lost along the way. My family, Billy, the Captain and the rest. It was too painful to think about and I knew that if I carried on this train of thought that it would cripple me for days. Right now, my friends needed me to be alert and stay on track. If we were to make this our new home then we needed to get more information from Mick; food and water supplies, how secure the place was etc. We needed to talk to the other members in our group to see how they felt about staying here.

So instead of dwelling in my feelings I buried them deep and focused on the fences that surrounded the entire area. We still had not checked the inside where they did most of the filming due to the weather in Wales being wet for most of the year.

Nia and Will broke off right to go and talk to the Snow's where they still sat, watching the children play in the park area. Heidi and Andrew Price were also sat adjacent to the Snow's watching their children.

I jogged a little to catch up with Adam and Amelia and the three of us approached Micks house together.

Before we could knock the door, it opened and we were faced with a tearful John.

"He's sick" he explained.

"Mick?" Amelia asked confused.

"Yeah, cancer. Said he was diagnosed before the outbreak and the last few weeks he's been getting worse. Ben has offered some pills to help him but he refused. Says we need to keep them" John staggered and Adam led him to a porch swing.

"What did you guys need?" John asked after a moment of trying to compose himself.

"We uh, found three trailers. One that will sleep six and another will sleep four. We wondered if the Snows could have the one and if Adam and I along with George, Nia and Will could take the bigger one?" Amelia asked, placing a hand on his shoulder.

"We also wanted to know about food rations and water. We don't have a lot left from what we brought from camp" I chipped in, sorry to be adding more questions and stress but we needed these decisions made as soon as possible.

John nodded, he looked tired.

"Take the Trailers, there's only Mick been living here and this is his place" John raised his hand to the house behind him. "Ben, Lewis, Cory and I will be staying here with Mick incase he gets any worse. Can you gather everyone in the house next door and I'll bring over some plans that Mick gave me?"

"Yep, I'm on it" I smiled and started to walk back towards the park, that's where I had seen the most of our people had gathered.

"Hey all, can you meet at house number two asap?"

People nodded and started to walk back towards the main entrance where the houses were situated.

I did another lap around the perimeter just in case I had missed anyone. I couldn't wait to see inside the building that held various sets.

When I entered the second house I was met by happy smiling faces, all chattering away, ecstatic about this new place.

John, Lewis and Cory entered the room, Cory went to play with the Prices kids who sent them outside to play.

"Right then, thanks everyone for coming" John spoke up, laying some plans on the huge dining room table.

The room got quiet very quickly. Everyone eager to hear what he had to say.

"Right, up until now, Mick was the only person staying at this place. He says that he's seen the odd zombie here and there but nothing he couldn't handle. The fences and gates were fortified to keep out fans and stalkers when the actors were here. There are three huge Winnebago's and three real houses. Each house has four bedrooms. We have the food that we brought and Mick says that there's a food van here which has cases of water and dried fruit packets. He isn't sure but he thinks that the food van has gas bottles to run the stove but he doesn't know if there is gas left in any of them. There is also a fully functioning well here for fresh water." He smiled widely at the last part.

This was an amazing find, a well. No more looking for water.

We could keep the crates of bottled water for when we went on supply runs etc.

"Ok, we can have some dinner together tonight and discuss who wants to live where and wait until morning to work out our rations. Is that ok with everyone?" Will asked.

They all nodded one by one, Mr. and Mrs. Snow hugged each other tightly. I smiled at Nia, hopefully this would be our forever home. I wouldn't allow myself to get my hopes up though, I'd thought that about our camp and look how that turned out.

Later that night we all had dinner together as Will had suggested. We pulled extra chairs and another table into the second house from the third one. It was the best night that I'd had in a while. In fact I think it was the best night that any of us had had in a long time.

We had fruit that Nia and Will had brought from camp, that was our starters. For our main we had some dried military meals and for dessert we each had a half a protein bar. The children had half a chocolate breakfast bar each. It was a lively evening with plenty of smiles and laughter.

Whilst the children played in the large back garden, us adults had a level headed, fair discussion on who was going to live where.

It was agreed that John, Lewis, Ben and Cory would stay at Micks place to keep an eye on him, Mr and Mrs Snow would take the smaller Winnebago with Maddy and Amber.

Nia, Will, Adam, Amelia and Myself would be in the larger Winnebago.

Heidi, Andrew and their kids would take the second house that we were having dinner in.

Brian and Sheila were going to take the third smaller trailer.

With the Prices permission, I took a wander around the house whilst everyone else played a game of eye spy with the kids. The house was all open plan. It had a large living area and dining room all fully furnished in plush, expensive furniture and accessories in cream and gold. The kitchen had grey cupboards and black counter tops and a double fridge which of course was no good to us now.

Upstairs there were four bedrooms, each with huge king-sized beds in them and two of which had en suite bathrooms. All covered in what looked like expensive bedding all in shades of White and Grey with accessories of lemon, lime and orange throughout. What a way to live, I walked out onto the balcony through the glass double doors in the master bedroom and sat on the white metal chair out there.

It looked out over the front of the house, I could see the park from where I was. It was quiet and peaceful, aside from the laughter and the voices of my friends down below. In this setting, it was easy to forget the horrors that lay outside these gates.

I must have been sat up there around twenty minutes when the hushed voices of Andrew and Heidi Price got louder, floating up the stairs.

Heidi poked her head through the door, she was carrying one of the smaller children. "We are just going to take the children to bed. It's been a long couple of days." She whispered and smiled.

"Thank you I'll head downstairs, if you need any help let me know." I followed her into the hallway. She carried on along it as I made my way down the stairs. Andrew came down just after me and ushered the older children up the stairs to bed also.

The rest of us waved and headed outside. We all gathered together and whispered our goodbyes. We headed to our trucks to get our bags. I was lucky that Nia and Will had picked up my bag before they had left. It held the picture that poppy had given me before I had left my home for what was supposed to have been a short-term supply run and also the photo album that I thought I'd lost forever.

They were my most prized possessions. I got them out of my bag and hugged them to my chest as we walked along quietly, back to the Winnebago.

Amelia and Adam took Mr and Mrs Snow or Ken and Rita as they had asked to be called, to their Winnebago and showed them and their granddaughters around.

Nia, Will and I carried on with Brian and Sheila to our new home. We hugged and waved goodbye to our new neighbours who were just on the other side of us.

Mr and Mrs Snow on the left, us in the middle and Brian and Sheila on the end. The end one was a smaller trailer and not a Winnebago as Mick had told us. It had a double bed and a double pull out in the lounge. Brian had offered to stay in the lounge as Sheila did not want to stay alone. That was the excuse but I'd seen the way that they looked at each other. I wasn't going to voice it out loud as it was their private business and I'm sure that they would tell us all if it got serious.

Nia and Will, got a bottle of water between them, one for Amelia and Adam to share and I got my own.

It hit me like a sledge hammer to the gut that I no longer had anyone to share my water with. I tried to smile through the pain but I could feel it bubbling up from my chest to my throat, threatening to burst free from my mouth. Spewing the hurt and rage like hot molten lava over my friends.

"I uh, I'm going to check the perimeter. See you in a bit" Nia gave me the look that she knew what I was thinking but she didn't say anything. They just let me leave. I walked slowly around the perimeter, the fence didn't have any gaps in it like the ones back at camp. Not even the gates at either end of the site had gaps. They had big white boards attached to them and barbed wire on the top. Everywhere I checked seemed secure, but as this was only day one I didn't want to get my hopes up.

CHAPTER FOURTEEN

I came across an area at the back of the compound, just behind the set that was kind of like a shelter. It had a back, top and sides, with slats that you could open and close, but no front. I wandered in curious as to what it had been used for, only to find some comfy looking leather bean bags, next to which were tall silver ashtrays. This was a smoking shed. There were outdoor electric heaters bolted to the ceiling which was painted a dark blue and had white and silver stars painted all over it; Mimicking the night sky. I lay back in one of the bean bags and looked at the fake sky. It was beautiful.

It was quite a warm evening and the bag I sat on was so comfortable that I could feel my eyes getting heavier. I let them drop, trying to block out the calls from the dead friends and family that kept trying to enter my thoughts. There was no room for the dead here, neither walking or otherwise. I needed some rest.

The next thing that I was aware of was Will's voice calling my name. "George? G man are you out here?" I could hear his footsteps getting closer, until he was just outside the glorified shed in which I sat.

"In here Will" I called out. Sitting up from where I was slouched, I stretched and yawned, it was a lot darker outside than it had been when I had first come in here. There were low beams of light outside from solar lights dotted around the site.

Will poked his head in and handed me a beer.

"Holy shit, where did you find a beer?" I asked, having fully believed that I would never see another beer ever again. I grinned so widely that my cheeks hurt.

"There were two six packs of bottles in the Snow's fridge and they brought them to us in case the girls found them first. I left the rest back at our trailer" he grinned. I never thought that I would see a bottle of beer ever again, not a full one anyway.

"Cheers" I held out the bottle and savoured the clink of the glass as Will knocked his against mine.

He had sat next to me on a multi coloured zig zag bean bag. "it's amazing in here" he gestured towards the ceiling. "I could kill for a cigarette right now"

"Me too and I've never smoked" I laughed, taking a long pull of my drink. It was warm but oh so good.

We sat there in comfortable silence, drinking our beer and looking up at the starry ceiling. I took small sips, trying to make it last.

"So, two six packs?" I questioned, holding up my bottle in awe.

"Yep, just stored in the fridge behind all the rotten food. We pulled out the beer and put the food back. The fridge is now sealed up."

"Then why the hell are we only having two" I joked.

Will laughed a deep belly chuckle. "Because my friend, Adam and Lewis also had one and because we should ration them. There are eight left."

"Not Mr snow? Or anyone else?" I questioned, knowing that Nia enjoyed a beer.

"Nope we asked everyone and they left them to us"

The sudden blaring of horns and men yelling caused us both to jump up and out of our seats.

"What the fuck is that? it'll bring every zombie for miles around this way." Will cursed.

We ran towards the main gate, my first thought was that somebody was in trouble and my second was that I should have brought my gun.

The Snows, Adam, Nia and Amelia were outside of our trailers. Brian was just coming out to see what was going on.

"What the hell is that?" Adam called out, jumping down the steps that led into our trailer.

"Everyone stay in doors for now." Will called as he kept running.

"Adam stay here and keep a watch over everyone, just in case get their weapons ready. Put all the kids and the Snow's into our trailer. Just for now ok?" I called out, not slowing down either.

Will got to the gate first and opened the peephole as quietly as possible.

"Come on Mick, you said you'd help us man, we even have an offering for you." Came a voice from the darkness.

I tapped Will lightly on the shoulder "What's up?"

"I see two trucks in front of the gate and what looks to be a car further back. They seem to be full but I can't really tell in this light." He whispered, not wanting to give away that we were watching them.

"Friendlies?" I asked, hoping that it was the case as I didn't want to fight anymore. I just wanted to have our first night in our new amazing home in peace.

"It's hard to tell" Wills face looked grim and I knew what he was thinking. That these were not friendlies at all.

"I'm going to get Adam and Lewis and check out the other gate. Keep an eye out here" he was off like a shot.

I took his place behind the gate and peeped through the hole. There were two men sitting on the bonnet of the vehicle smoking whilst another urinated over the back tyre.

The two on the bonnet talked amongst themselves but so quietly that I couldn't hear what they were saying. The one on the left, looked tall and muscular, his hair looked to be back in a hair tie and he had a large bushy brown beard to match the colour of his hair.

"Come on Mick, it's me Jed, I'm losing patience here." He said sliding off the bonnet and sauntering towards the gate.

I shuffled my feet not realising how close to the gate my right foot was and I kicked it causing a giant clang.

"Oh, so you are there Mick? Well for not answering me I'll give you your present and then take it away."

"Richard, get her" Jed called out.

The guy at the back of the car, had finished urinating and was doing up his trousers. He gave Jed an evil smile and nodded, walking to the truck behind.

"Lee, get ready to ram that gate." he spoke to the man still sat on the bonnet who jumped off and sauntered back to the driver's side and into the seat.

Upon hearing footsteps behind me I turned to see Will, alone. He carried two handguns, I guessed that one was mine.

"You know, for an old guy you sure do move fast" I whispered.

He clipped me across the back of the head but before he could reply, the guy shouted out again

"Come on Mick, I know that you're familiar with this one" I heard a woman cry out.

Looking back through the small hole I saw the man they called Richard shoving a woman so hard that she staggered and fell.

"Come now Mick! We only want to share that lovely looking camp of yours" Jed called.

"Please just let me go" she begged.

Richard grabbed her roughly by the hair and placed a large knife against her throat.

Blood and Dirt streaked her face and clothes.

"Oh no" I whispered moving from the peephole so that Will could look.

"Amy" I whispered, my mind racing to catch up with what my eyes were seeing.

Before even thinking about it I started to pull open the first lock on the gate.

"No!" Mick was standing on his porch, well being held up by John and Ben anyway. He wore blue striped pyjamas that reminded me of a book that I read when I was younger. Cory peeked out from behind John.

"But they have-" Mick cut me off again.

"No Please" he was getting out of breath, the warning in Bens eyes was enough. Mick was weak and this stress was not helping.

I wanted to save Amy but I also wanted to respect Mick. After all this was his place. I would go and let him know about Amy and plead my case. I placed the bolt securely back across then followed Will over to Micks.

"Listen Mick he has a woman out there from our old camp. He's threatening her with a knife. God knows what he's capable of"

"Oh, I know exactly what he's capable of. Robert is my brother and Amy is my ex-wife"

"Then why the hell aren't we letting them in?" I asked utterly confused.

"Because my brother is a serial killer" Mick told us grimly.

I started to laugh, this was just completely insane and had to be some kind of sick joke. Perhaps to test us on our loyalty to him and this place?

"I'm serious, before this Jed was in a home for the criminally insane. He escaped during the confusion of the outbreak. I think that it was just pure luck that he found me or is even still alive, he never was the brightest but he is evil." Mick started to cough uncontrollably.

"I have to take him back indoors, he's not well enough for this" Ben told us.

"Ok let's get him inside"

"don't...open...cough...Gate...Cough" Mick gasped out before being led away.

Will and I walked back to the gate quietly.

I took the peephole as he climbed a tall ladder to the side of the gate. There were a few large planks of wood that it was leaning against. It seemed that Mick had been trying to build a platform.

I watched amused, as Will tried to balance his huge frame without revealing himself to the men below.

"What will it be Mick? Let us in or Amy loses her head." Jed's voice brought my attention back to what was happening outside the walls.

"See Mick isn't here at the moment and sorry to say that we don't have any room for more people." I was hoping that by informing him that Mick wasn't here then he would let Amy go.

"We have no need for her then" he nodded to Amy and gave Richard a pointed look.

"Wait! There's no need for anyone to get hurt. You go on your way and just leave the woman there. She can find her own way." I tried to reason with them.

Adam and Lewis came up on either side of me as backup, guns at the ready.

I would have loved to have pulled open the gate and let them lose on the bastards outside but we didn't know how many people were in the trucks behind and which of those were innocents.

"You're right there's no need for anyone to get hurt. But

asshole, we've seen inside those fences of yours and we want a slice of the safety. We are willing to do whatever it takes to get inside and that includes violence." Was the reply I got.

I watched as he gave Richard a thumb up. Richard pulled Amy's head back even further with his hand wrapped tightly in her hair and dragged his knife across her throat. Blood flowed freely down her throat and soaked onto her once light pink top.

"No!" I called out hitting the gate with the palm of my hand in anger.

I closed my eyes trying to rid the sight from my mind but I couldn't get away from the gurgling sounds as she choked on her own blood.

Will came down the ladder fast. "Hey guys, we have a load of zombies, I'd say at least three dozen coming this way."

"Oh shit, what do we do?" Adam looked worried.

"Round up all of the able adults. Get Mr and Mrs Snow over to the Price's and keep all of the children there, with Heidi. Let John stay with Mick but get Ben out here. We may need all hands available."

Adam nodded and ran back towards the trailers, Lewis towards his new house without another word.

"So what's it going to be? Are we just going to stand here all night taking out more and more people." Jed called.

Will put his finger to his lips asking me to be quiet and hopped back up the ladder. After a few moments he pointed to his eyes and then to me, then back outside.

I looked through the peephole, it took me a few moments to work out what he was showing me. Then I saw them. Dark shadows moving towards us like a huge black wall of death and decay.

I looked to see if any of the men outside had noticed but they were too caught up in attacking us.

Before they had murdered Amy in cold blood I may have warned them so that they would have gotten a fighting chance.

Now I hoped that every one of them would get what they deserved, I just hoped that the innocent people would not get hurt also. That they could make a run for it.

Richard had gone to the back of the truck to pull out another woman. Annabelle.

Her tear streaked face pulled at my heart as Amy's had earlier. Amy, I looked to where they had let her fall, blood turning the concrete a crimson slab.

Her hand twitched, did they know anything about zombies at all, the idiots.

What the hell had happened back at our old camp? How had Annabelle and Amy come to be hostages with these assholes?

"Please just let all your hostages go, I'm sure there are plenty of other places that have room for you" I called out, I looked up for Will but he had disappeared. I had no idea where, I hadn't even seen him come down the ladder.

I looked behind me but still couldn't see any sign of him, Adam had not returned either. John and Lewis came quietly out of their house and jogged towards me.

"G, Adam just radioed, they are covering the other gate just in case our friends out there get a little creative. Where's Will?" Lewis asked peeking through the hole and shaking his head in dismay at what he saw.

"I have no idea, one minute he was up there and the next, poof" I tried to explain.

The men outside had gone quiet, I spied back through the hole. They were huddled together, whispering. No doubt about how they were going to ram the gates.

Something at the back of their trucks caught my eye and I feared that the zombies were closer than we had thought. But it was Will and Adam, something must have told him that I could see them because Will looked at me and winked. They were leading another two women away from the trucks and around to the side of our compound. I assumed that they were bringing them in through our back gate. It was a risky move but the outcome outweighed those odds.

Now we just had to get Annabelle away from them. I had no idea how to do that without shooting at them and then possibly hitting her in the crossfire.

I had turned to talk with Lewis to see if he had any ideas when we heard Jed yell. "Ahhhhh get it off me"

I jumped, heart in my mouth my pulse raced faster.

I looked back through the gate to see Amy, now one of the undead, with her mouth clamped firmly around Jed's ankle, trying to tear through his trousers to get to the juicy flesh below.

Her skin had turned a mottled grey and her eyes now just two white orbs.

Richard put his gun to Amy's head and pulled the trigger, once again Amy's body slumped to the ground. This time she would not be getting back up again.

Rest in peace Amy, I'm sorry I couldn't save you. I sent up a silent prayer to the higher powers that they take her in with Kelly and the kids and look after them all.

"Aw hell thanks ma-" Jed's thanks were cut short by Richard putting his gun on Jed's head and pulling the trigger for the second time. Blood, Brain matter and bits of bone flew as the bullet exited Jed's skull.

"What the hell man?" the driver of the first car got out, followed by two men from the second truck. As far as I could tell nobody had gotten out of the third car.

Annabelle used the drama to run around the corner to where Will had taken the other two women. I hoped that they all got to safety.

The men did not notice too caught up in their own worries.

"He had been bitten" Richard said shrugging his shoulders. As if shooting a friend was a normal, easy-to-do kind of thing.

The driver thought about it for a moment or two and then also shrugged and nodded his head. Easily accepting the fate of his fallen leader.

I suppose these days, shooting a friend was normal to some, but for me I don't think that it would ever be easy.

"Hey fellas, you didn't tell us that you were bringing more friends" I pointed to the zombies that were closing in around them. I tried to sound cocky and confident, but my insides were rolling around like I'd just gotten off the world's largest and fastest roller coaster.

Watching Amy die and then return as one of those things, a fate that she did not deserve was not something I'd ever want to see any of my friends become.

"Good luck with this asshole, we will return. See you in a while, if there's anything left of you" Richard called. I watched them jump into their cars and reverse, taking out a few zombies on their way but leaving most of them for us to deal with. Then Richard and his crew were gone. The puffs of dirt in the air and the crimson stained floor the only indicators that anyone had ever been there.

My relief at their retreat was short lived however as it seemed like there were a lot more zombies than Will had estimated.

I heard a small buzz coming up behind me and turned to see Will and Adam coming towards us in a golf cart.

"Nice, we may need that as a getaway soon" I joked. Trying to make myself feel better. It didn't work.

Before anybody could reply, Ben came running out of Mick's house and towards us, calling out "Mick had an idea!"

CHAPTER FIFTEEN

"Ok, tell us" Will said eagerly, I guess that he was all out of ideas, just like me.

"Mick says there's a hill about twenty minutes West of here in a truck. On top of that hill is a hut but surrounding that hut is an extremely deep moat. The bridge is activated by remote. It was used for filming" Ben told us excitedly.

"Ok and how does this help us?" I was too tired and too horrified by the nights events to think clearly enough.

"Mick has volunteered to use the back gate to drive out of here and around the front making as much noise as he can to draw the zombies that way. He will cross the bridge and lead the zombies to fall into the moat"

"How did he even know about the zombies?" Adam asked

"He's been watching out of his bedroom window using a telescope. The plan he's been thinking about for weeks just in case he ever had to leave here." Ben explained.

"No not Mick, he's too ill. I will go." Will said firmly.

"It's because he's not well that he's chosen to go. In all honesty, he won't last long here. We don't have any way to help him. He had stage three lung cancer even before the outbreak and was given six months so he's living borrowed time. I have to agree with him on this, he would be our best hope." Ben told us, a grim look on his face.

"How's John?" Lewis asked looking towards the house from which Ben had just came. As soon as the men had retreated, John had gone back home to sit with his dying friend.

"He argued at first, but he can see the sense of it." Ben replied

"Lewis come in, you there man?" came the voice of Andrew via the radio.

"Yeah, I'm here, what's up?"

"I have an idea, meet me in the stunt set. First large building you come to." That was all he said, but the excitement in his voice was hard to miss. It had us all intrigued.

"Ok, I'll stay here with Adam, and keep an eye on them," Will pointed outside of the gate. "G, you go with Lewis and check out what Andrew has found."

"Ok no worries, I'd wondered where Andrew had disappeared to,"

"Ben can you go back in and check on Mick and John?" Lewis asked.

We each nodded and made our way quickly to where we needed to be.

Lewis and I jogged over to the stunt set, although I'd seen it from the exterior on my walk earlier that evening I hadn't entered any of the buildings. I was going to save that for the next day.

Andrew was already at the door waiting for us. His eyes shone with excitement.

"Come on you two, I have something awesome to show you," and he was gone, back into the darkness.

My eyes met Lewis's, he just shrugged and disappeared through the door.

I followed quickly knowing that time was of the essence.

The place was huge, with cameras and computers every-where, there were green screens dotted all over the place in various sizes.

"Wow this place is awesome," I marveled as I turned around in circles. Soft lights were on in here, I wasn't sure why, maybe some sort of security measure running on a generator. I made a note to ask Mick about it later.

"You think that's cool? You should see this!" Andrews voice came from somewhere to my right.

I followed the sound of excited voices further into the room and into what looked like a huge storage room.

"Check this out!" now it was Lewis's turn to sound excited.

I didn't see what the big deal was, they were stood in front of a Porsche 911. Don't mistake me, it was a stunning looking car, it had been painted in a deep purple, that seemed to shimmer. But we had bigger, sturdier cars out front that would hold up much better in the horde of zombies that we currently had surrounding the compound.

"And?" I was at a loss.

"Man, it's a full sized remote-control car. Don't you see?" Lewis was looking at me as though I was dumb and in this instance, I was being real slow on the uptake.

"No," I walked closer, foolishly thinking that by getting nearer I might have worked out what they were so excited about.

"We can control it from here. We can use the camera booms to get up high then use the remote car to draw the zombies away and into that pit Mick was talking about." Lewis piped up.

Andrew was nodding along like one of those dogs you used to see in car windows.

Now I saw what they were getting at, I realised how great this find was, and then I had an idea.

"This is great, make your way around to the back gate, I'll

meet you there in a few." I ran back out the way I had come and towards the food van.

Jimmying the lock on the back of the trailer that was attached to the van I gagged at the rancid odour of rotten meat. No generator for this then. Holding my nose, I took deep breaths in through my mouth.

I didn't have to hold it for long as the item I was after was lined neatly by the door. There were six of them. I pulled out one and found out exactly how heavy they were. But that was good as it meant that they were full. A lot of huffing and puffing later, I had manged to get three of them off the trailer and had wedged the door closed.

The whir of the golf cart had me thanking the heavens for small things. John and Mick came slowly towards me, both with grim faces.

"What you up to George?" John asked pulling to a stop just in front of me.

"Yes son, I think you're on to something there," Mick grinned at me. I couldn't help but grin back. I hurriedly ran through my plan as I put the gas canisters in the back where the clubs would normally be.

John seemed to like it, Mick remained quiet. I hopped on the back to hold the canisters whilst john drove us to meet Lewis and Andrew.

"The car works great," Andrew called out.

"Ah this beauty, I'd forgotten she was here." Mick said shakily getting out of the cart and hobbling over to the car. He tried to open the door but didn't seem to have the strength. I trotted up behind him and opened it for him.

"Thanks," he mumbled and got into the driver's seat.

"Guys," I gestured with my hands that they join me at the back of the car.

They did, Will and Adam jogging up just as I'd started to speak.

"Ok here's my plan. Andrew gets up on the camera boom over on the left wall there." I pointed roughly to where he could stand.

"Then he controls the car leading the zombies away. When he's far enough away he can crash and boom," I pointed to the gas bottles.

The group started to nod.

"But there's no guarantee that the canisters will blow? Or to how far the remote will work in the car." Will, found two major flaws in our plan. Even Andrew looked dejected.

"No, it's a good plan," Mick piped up still in the Porsche. "But instead of remote I'll be driving it," he grinned madly and I think that he was looking forward to going out with a bang; no pun intended.

"But Mick–" John started, I could hear the pain in his voice.

"But Mick nothing, you know I'm a goner anyway. I'm just an old man living on borrowed time. If I can help you guys and those lil ones back at the house then I will." Mick had a no nonsense look on his face and his tone warned not to argue.

John opened his mouth as if to argue but closed it again when Mick slammed the door to the Porsche closed. Damn for a man with no strength he sure did slam the door hard.

He held out his hand to Lewis who now held the remote. He looked to John who just looked to the floor. Mick cleared his throat loudly and Lewis quickly handed him the keys, looking like a guilty school boy.

"Mick, thank you," I tried to sound as sincere as I could. There was nothing more to say. Words could not have expressed how grateful I was to this man. He had only known our group for less than a day but was willing to give up his life for us, when he could have been living out his last days in the luxury of his home.

He just nodded grimly and saluted us. John stumbled to the

car, unable to see properly in his grief. He hugged Mick tightly and whispered his goodbyes.

"It's clear." Will called, he was checking through the back gate to make sure that out there wasn't zombie infested also.

"It's time." Mick called out, a slight tremor in his voice giving away the fact that he was a little scared. But then again when driving to certain death, what man wouldn't be a scared.

He started the engine with a roar, Lewis, Adam and Will gave him a little nod as they quickly pulled open the gate. John and I got our guns at the ready just as a cover in case there were any stray zombies about.

Mick didn't waste any time. He put his foot down and the engine roared, speeding out of the compound.

"Woohoo," we could hear Micks excited scream. He really did love the car.

Will, Adam and Lewis pulled the heavy gate closed again as quickly as they could, I kept my gun pointed at them just in case and John ran to the golf cart and was gone before we could stop him.

My eyes met Lewis' panicked look.

"Go," I told him, and he was gone at a run, no questions asked. Andrew followed quickly behind with a small wave to us, probably going to check on Heidi and the kids.

I put my gun in my belt and ran towards the gate, helping Will and Adam to pull it fully closed and lock it back up securely.

"Let's hope it works," he said looking through the peephole out into the darkness.

"Yeah," I nodded we turned to walk back towards home and the main entrance.

By the time we got there, John was up on top of the ladder that Will had vacated with a pair of binoculars.

The horn from the car blared, "Come on suckers, come get

me you filthy rotten animals," could be heard in between horn blasts.

I had to smile at Mick, he really was giving it his all.

"It's working." John called down quietly.

"I'm just going to check on Cory," Lewis replied.

"I'll go check on the girls," Will told me, clapping me on the back.

"Me too," Adam gave his goofy grin. I smiled back, warmth filling me inside.

"I'm going to wait here for a little while," I nodded up at John, the blaring of the horn was getting quieter now as Mick moved away.

I checked through the small hole in the gate and saw that our plan seemed to be working, the zombies had turned away from us and were following the sound of the car which I could no longer see.

Hope filled me, with just a small niggle in the back of my mind that hoped the noise didn't draw more zombies towards us than it did away.

About thirty minutes later there was crackle on Johns radio which was turned down low.

We were now sat side by side on the ground in front of the gate, each exhausted and nodding off. Sleep threatening to take me over completely, despite the nap I had taken earlier in the smoking shed.

"Hey, it's Mick." his voice sounded raspy but it could have just been the signal.

"Mick, it's me John, how are you man?" John's tone was rushed, he was worried about his friend and rightly so.

"I'm as good as can be. I've made it into the hut and have pulled up the bridge. It seems to be working, they are still coming at me and falling into the moat." He chuckled, followed by a chesty cough.

"That's good Mick. But, how are you?" John stressed the last word.

"I'm ok son, I'll give it an hour. I have the car idling with the cd player running, to hopefully draw more in."

"Thank you, Mick, I wish there had been another way," John dipped his head, I watched as silent tears hit the dirt in between his legs.

Placing my hand on his shoulder I took the radio off him.

"Hey, Mick it's me, George. Thanks again man, you've saved our lives today. Is there anything we can do for you?"

"Hey George, nope I'm all good. Just look after John there. I'm going to keep a little battery in this thing. Over and out," he chuckled at the last bit and didn't wait for my reply before turning his radio off.

"Want to go in?" I asked John quietly, keeping hold of the radio.

"Nah, not just yet. Can we just sit here for a while?" he sniffed, lifting his red, bloodshot eyes to meet mine. Almost pleading with me silently. My heart went out to him, we'd all lost our fair share of loved ones. Me? Well I'd had more than my fair share of loved and lost. I don't think I could handle anymore loss at the moment or ever again.

I just nodded, he lay his head on my shoulder and I placed mine back against the gate. The night was relatively warm and it wasn't long before I could feel my eyes starting to close again, John's soft snores alerted me that he was sleeping and soon they lulled me to sleep.

CHAPTER SIXTEEN

The low rumble of a small explosion jolted us awake. We were both on our feet within seconds, my heart was beating so hard I thought my ribs were going to break.

"What the hell?" John was scrambling up the ladder as I fumbled with the latches that held the peephole closed. My fingers were numb and not working properly.

"No, no no. Please God no," John begged the invisible higher power.

I finally got the cover open and looked through. A plume of smoke rose in the distance. So, my idea of the gas canisters worked. I was both happy that I helped even a little but I had what felt like a large lead weight in my stomach. Another life lost. How many more would we lose before we won this war? Would we ever win this war?

I watched as John slid down the ladder and snatched up the radio from where it had fallen to the ground when we were sleeping.

"Mick? You there? Come in Mick please?" John spoke into the radio but only got static in return.

"I'm sorry John, he seemed like a good man," I walked to my

friend and hugged him tight. My arms barely reaching around his muscular frame.

"He really was," Johns voice broke and his shoulders slumped against me, his legs barley holding him up.

"Come on let's get you into Lewis," I let him go and wrapped my arm around his shoulder, steering John towards his new home.

I saw him inside; Lewis and Cory were curled up in the corner of the massive U shaped black fabric sofa. They had pulled one of the grey tartan throws from the back of the sofa over them.

Lewis stirred as we entered the room, his eye met mine. I shook my head no. He closed his eyes briefly, then untangled himself from the young boy that they had adopted as their own.

I helped John to sit down on the opposite end of the sofa. Lewis moved to join him, not saying a word, just hugging his partner.

I grabbed the other throw and handed it to them, placing a hand on each shoulder. Not saying anything, there was nothing to say. Mick was an amazing man, who had selflessly given his life for us and our group. Words could never express the sympathy I had for John or the appreciation I felt for Mick.

But there was a time and place for those comments. Right at that moment I knew that John just needed Lewis to hug him tight throughout the night; giving him comfort that nobody else could.

I moved silently throughout their home into the large kitchen/diner. Picking up two bottles of water from the worktop I was a little surprised to see that they were flavoured water. Good old Mick. Nothing but the best for him and now for our good friends. Both the bottles were still, Lemon and Lime flavoured. I wasn't sure if John and Lewis would like it but then again we couldn't really afford to be picky these days; any water as long as it was clean was good.

Placing the bottles on the small wooden coffee table in front of the sofa, I earned small smiles from both men.

"I'll see myself out, goodnight both. Should you need anything, you know where we are." I whispered.

Whispers of thanks from both of them saw me out of the door.

I strolled home, the sun was starting to come up. I looked forward to getting into my bed. It had been a long ass night.

I climbed the steps to the trailer and opened the door as quietly as I could.

Nia and Will were both propped against each other sleeping. They were sat on the sofa that was my pull-out bed.

I decided to sleep in Will's bed for the night, or day as the case was. The front door clicked loudly behind me, causing me to cringe. I didn't want to wake them, they too had experienced a long couple of days.

Too late, they both woke up, stretching and yawning. Both blessing me with small smiles, when they laid eyes on me.

"Sorry," I scrunched up my face trying to look sorry.

"Nah man, that's ok." Will grinned.

"We were trying to wait up for you. I've left a few blankets and pillows just there for you." Nia smiled and pointed to a pile of dark coloured bedding on the chair opposite.

"Thanks," I yawned, desperate to snuggle up warm and close my eyes.

"Mick?" Will asked.

"No." that's all I needed to say.

They both looked down to the floor, feeling the loss of Mick.

"Hey, you two. Get to bed and let's get some proper rest,"

Nia nodded, she got up sluggishly. Giving me a hug before slinking off to her room without another word.

"You stay with John and Lewis?" Will asked also standing

up. His top and joggers creased badly from falling asleep in them.

"Lewis went inside to put Cory to sleep. I stayed outside the gates with John waiting to hear off Mick. We fell asleep sat on the ground. I just took John home and made sure he was ok," I explained.

"You're a good man G." Will hugged me tightly too.

"Where are Annabelle and the other women I saw you saving?" I'd completely forgotten about them with all of the drama regarding Mick.

"They are ok, a little shaken up but they will bounce back. For now we've put them in with Sheila and Brian." he smiled a tight smile.

"I'm so glad that Annabelle is safe, Will, but I can't believe that Amy is gone," my old friend guilt was clawing its way back into my stomach and chest, causing me to feel nauseous.

"Hey, don't even think about blaming yourself for that one ok? If we had given in and opened that gate then who knows how many of us would still be standing here right now," Will looked me in the eye "Would you have wanted to subject Nia, Amelia and the others to a man like Jed? It would be Deacons place all over again. We fought so hard to leave there."

"I know, I know. I would never want anyone to go through that again. Thank you Will," I let out a huge sigh. Just because I understood why we didn't open the gates to save Amy, didn't mean that I had to like it.

"You're Welcome G. Now get some rest. We shall meet with everyone tomorrow afternoon to plan our stay here."

"Good night Will," I replied hugging him again, clapping his back a few times.

He gave me a warm smile before also heading to his room.

I watched after him for a little while, feeling grateful that I still had people left in this world who I loved and who loved me. I was wrong to try to push them away. I should have been pulling them closer, making every second count, because these days we never knew when it would be our last.

Another long yawn showed me just how much my body needed to rest. I stripped down to my navy t shirt and orange boxer shorts. Pulled out the sofa bed easily and grabbed the navy cotton blankets, quilt, along with the fluffy pillows dressed in a bright yellow that Nia had left out for me.

Lying back, I was surprised at how comfortable the sofa bed was, that added with the warmth of the blankets and quilt and the softness of the pillows had me drowsy once more. Only then realizing just how tired and worn down I really was.

I closed my eyes and tried to focus on the good things in my past. Meeting Kelly, getting married, the births of our children. Poppy's first day at school (Kelly and I had booked the day off to take her), Cameron going to swimming lessons and dropping his float, my heart nearly exploded when he disappeared under the water. But the lifeguards were excellent, bringing him back to the surface, coughing and spluttering whilst also giving me the thumbs up that he was ok. Then meeting my extended family, Will, Nia, Adam, Billy, Amelia, John and Lewis. Hopefully the Snow's, Price's, Brian, Sheila and Annabelle too. To Lieutenant Daniel Jacks, I offered up a silent prayer that he stay safe and hopefully make his way back to us.

I would do anything to protect these people. Mick had seen the same special, unique thing in our bunch of misfits that I had. They were strong, kind, loving, incredible people. Worth dying for any day.

I think Kelly and the kids would have loved our group of people.

I lay there for a little while longer before going to sleep. Dreaming about all the incredible possibilities that lay in the long road ahead.

The End

ABOUT THE AUTHOR

Website
Reader Group

Printed in Great Britain
by Amazon